Dear George Clooney

DEAR
GEORGE
CLOONEY
PLEASE MARRY MY MOM

Susin Nielsen

Tundra Books

First paperback edition published by Tundra Books, 2012

Published in Canada by Tundra Books,
75 Sherbourne Street, Toronto, Ontario M5A 2P9

Published in the United States by Tundra Books of Northern New York,
P.O. Box 1030, Plattsburgh, New York 12901

Library of Congress Control Number: 2009938090

Library and Archives Canada Cataloguing in Publication

Nielsen-Fernlund, Susin, 1964-
Dear George Clooney, please marry my mom / Susin Nielsen.

ISBN 978-1-77049-295-0

I. Title.

PS8577.I37D43 2011 jC813'.54 C2011-901404-1

We acknowledge the financial support of the Government of Canada through the Canada Book Fund and that of the Government of Ontario through the Ontario Media Development Corporation's Ontario Book Initiative.

We further acknowledge the support of the Canada Council for the Arts and the Ontario Arts Council for our publishing program.

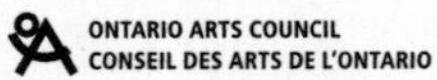

Design: Kelly Hill

Typeset in Scala

Printed and bound in the United States of America

1 2 3 4 5 6 17 16 15 14 13 12

To all of my family members
– Nielsen, Fernlund, Inkster, and Dixon –
I'm blessed to have you in my life.

Acknowledgments

Thank you to my son, Oskar, and my husband, Goran, for being early readers and for giving excellent (and brutally honest) critiques. To the team at Tundra: Kelly Hill for another wonderful cover; Sue Tate, who expertly helped me get rid of the potholes; and especially Kathy Lowinger, who saw the diamond in the rough and who worked tirelessly to help me tell the story I wanted to tell and tell it well.

Thanks also to my agent, Hilary McMahon, for her passion, kindness, and smarts.

Author's Note

I've now managed to write two books in a row that feature single moms with erratic behavior. I must clarify that they are nothing like my own mom. Mom, you were a single parent, but you were, and are, a rock, and I love you more than I can express.

The hair design school in this book is named after my dear friend Will Berto. Will, you left us far too early, but you live on in the hearts and minds of all of your friends. I love you and miss you.

Finally – with the exception of the underwear-flushing incident – this is entirely a work of my imagination. However, if George Clooney would ever like to meet to discuss any aspects of this novel, I'll drop everything and be right over.

DEAR
GEORGE
CLOONEY
PLEASE MARRY MY MOM

— I —

FOR THE RECORD: I did not mean to send my two half sisters to the emergency room.

What happened was this: Rosie – my whole sister – and I were in Los Angeles for our second annual Fake Christmas. Real Christmas had already been celebrated in Vancouver with Mom. Fake Christmas took place on the twenty-seventh of December with Dad. I called it that because everything about it, from the date to the tree to Jennica's boobs, was phony.

But the presents weren't. They were real, and there were lots of them. Rosie got a talking doll and a fairy costume and computer games and the Playmobil grocery-store set she'd always wanted, but that Mom couldn't afford. It came with tiny plastic cucumbers and apples and beans and bananas, which you could stack on a tiny stand, and four plastic people. Even I liked it, and I'm practically a teenager.

I got an iPod Touch and two new pairs of Converse high tops. The first pair was a Chuck Taylor design, with roses and skulls painted all over the fabric; the second pair was black leather. They were awesome. I also got a skirt from Jennica, which I would never wear because I never wear skirts – only jeans and T-shirts – which you'd think she would have figured out by now.

Lola and Lucy got a bunch of presents too, even though they'd already been given tons of gifts when they'd celebrated their own Real Christmas. Jennica didn't want them to feel left out.

I won't lie, the gift-opening part of our visit was fun.

The weird part had been the so-called surprise.

My dad had picked us up at LAX that morning, looking tanned and buff. "I have a surprise for you girls," he'd said as we got on the freeway. For a fleeting, insane, Pollyanna moment, I actually thought he was going to tell us he was dumping Jennica and coming back to Vancouver.

But, instead, he drove us to Santa Monica, a beautiful neighborhood near the ocean. He pulled into the driveway of a sprawling, modern ranch-style house with a lush garden.

"Like it? It's ours."

I understood that by *ours,* he didn't really mean *ours.*

"Wow," said Rosie, drawing out the word, her five-year-old self unable to keep the awe out of her voice.

"What happened to the condo in Burbank?" I asked.

Dad shrugged. "It was getting a little tight for the four of us. Plus it was a rental."

The new house was beautiful. It was big. The porch didn't sag, the gutters weren't broken, and I was pretty sure the roof didn't need replacing.

It was nothing like our house in Vancouver.

I was trying to think of something mean to say when Wife Number Two dashed outside and hugged us.

"Girls, it's so lovely to see you!" Jennica said, and I was reminded all over again that she was a lousy actress. "I like your hair, Violet. It's pretty when it's a bit longer." I made a silent vow to ask my mom to cut it short again when we got home.

The twins were having their nap, so Dad and Jennica toured us through the house. All the rooms were on one floor, but it was a gigantic floor. I hardly recognized any of the furniture. "Our old stuff just didn't suit this place," Jennica told us, running her hand through her long blonde hair. "Plus this house is *soooo* much bigger than the condo."

They walked us through the living room, with its sleek modern couches in shades called *mocha* and *taupe,* and into the bright, airy kitchen with its stainless steel appliances. Then they showed us the bedrooms, at the far end of the house. The master bedroom was huge, with a king-sized bed and a walk-in closet that was as big as the room Rosie and I shared at home, but without the sloped ceilings. My dad's clothes took about one-eighth of the space – the rest of the closet was stuffed full of Jennica's things. She had more clothes than my mom, Rosie, and me put together.

The twins shared the room next to Dad and Jennica's. Jennica opened the door quietly so we could peek inside. "I wanted it to look like a fairy tale," she whispered.

The twins were fast asleep, sprawled out on two matching canopy beds, safety bars in place so they wouldn't roll out. The canopies and duvets were covered in shimmering pink fabric. *Princess Lola* was written in silver above one bed, *Princess Lucy* above the other. A window seat was filled with pink and silver cushions. Stars and moons had been stenciled all over the ceiling. Built-in shelves held all their toys.

"And here's your room," Jennica said, sweeping her arm toward the door at the end of the hallway like Vanna White on the "Wheel of Fortune." The beige walls were bare except for a bland watercolor of a sunset that hung between the IKEA-brand twin beds.

When the twins woke up, we unwrapped presents in the new living room, sitting on the floor by the fake tree. It was only three o'clock in the afternoon when we were done, so Dad took us outside. The backyard was even bigger than the front. It had a swing set, a playground-sized sandbox, and a kidney-shaped pool surrounded by a fence.

Our yard in Vancouver had a rusted trampoline with a broken leg. And mud.

"I didn't know Jennica liked to garden," I said to my dad, as I took in all the colorful flowers and plants.

He laughed. "She doesn't. The garden was here when we bought the place. Fortunately, our nanny has a green thumb."

I'd forgotten about the nanny.

"It's a bit too cold for swimming," Dad said. "Why don't you play in the sandbox?"

As an almost-teenager, this hardly appealed to me, but Rosie and the twins loved the idea, so we dragged the lid off the sandbox and piled in. Lola and Lucy were so cute, it hurt. They were just under two years old, and they'd inherited the best of their parents' genes: Jennica's thick blonde hair and big brown eyes, and my dad's chin dimple and megawatt smile.

Rosie and I hadn't been nearly as lucky in the gene-pool lottery. Despite having the same father and a very attractive mother, all we'd inherited was Dad's mousy brown hair and his poor eyesight. He wore contacts; we wore glasses. I'd managed to get his big feet and ears, too, and his bulbous man-knees. All these things looked good on my dad, but transplanted onto a scrawny girl like me, it was seriously unfortunate.

We played with the twins for a long time in that sandbox. They adored being with Rosie and me, and I would have loved them with all my heart if I hadn't hated them so much.

After dinner we hung out in the family room, which was just as big as the living room, but more casual. Dad was on the couch reading the paper, but when Lucy and Lola crawled up beside him, he put the paper down and scooped them both into his arms, calling them "my little starbursts" and tickling them until they were giggling uncontrollably, a mass of little limbs.

Rosie sat nearby watching, her lips pursed.

When Jennica took the twins away so she could give them their bath, Rosie launched herself at him. "Daddy!" she shouted, jumping onto his lap.

"Ow!" Dad exclaimed. "Rosie, holy cow, you've gotten big! Sit beside me, okay? You're too heavy for my lap." He picked her up and placed her beside him. Then he picked up his newspaper and started reading again.

Rosie's bottom lip quivered, but she didn't say a word.

"Violet, I almost forgot," my dad said from behind the sports section. "Do you mind going out and putting the lid on the sandbox? Our neighbors on both sides have cats."

"Sure thing," I said. I got up and left the room. But instead of going outside, I snuck into Dad and Jennica's enormous en-suite bathroom and had a pee and didn't flush.

At bedtime, Rosie made me guard the door while she put on a pair of pull-ups under her pajamas.

"You won't tell anyone, will you?" she asked, her thumb slipping into her mouth.

I pulled her thumb out. "Never."

"Cross your heart, hope to die, stick a needle in your eye?"

"All that."

The next morning after breakfast, the twins wanted to go back to the sandbox. I held on to their chubby little hands and led them outside, Rosie following a few steps behind. Dad and Wife Number Two stayed in the kitchen, drinking their lattes.

We'd been playing for only a few minutes when Lola asked, "What dat?" She pointed at two big cat turds half-buried in the sand.

FOR THE RECORD: I'm not proud of what I did next. But I also don't think it called for the freak-out that followed.

What happened was this: When Rosie started to answer, I clamped my hand over her mouth. "It's chocolate," I said. "Santa must have left it. Look, there's one for each of you."

The twins reached into the sand. They picked up the turds. They popped them into their mouths. They chewed. They swallowed.

They burst into tears.

Dad and Jennica were outside in a flash. When she found out what had happened (thanks to Rosie, who couldn't tell a lie save her life), Jennica wanted Dad to call 911. Seriously. He made her see reason, sort of, and the two of them drove the twins to the nearest hospital instead. Don't ask me what she thought an ER doctor could do. Maybe give the twins some high-powered mouthwash.

Rosie and I were left alone in the house for over two hours. We went into the family room and turned on the flat-screen TV.

I knew I was in big trouble. I knew Mom would hear about it. And I knew I should feel bad about what I'd done.

But I didn't. I felt empty – like if you looked inside me at that moment, there'd be nothing there. Just a great big blank.

About fifteen minutes into a rerun of *Arthur,* Rosie

said, "You never made *me* eat poo." Her eyes didn't leave the TV.

"No, Rosie," I said, gently pulling her thumb out of her mouth and taking her hand in mine. "And I never would."

Jennica wouldn't even look at me when they got home. That night I heard Dad on the phone to my mom, telling her about my "ongoing troubling behavior." The next morning, I announced that I'd like to go back to Vancouver. Nobody argued. Rosie didn't want to leave, but she was too young to travel by herself, so she had to come with me. I packed up all our clothes and all our new gifts, except for the skirt, which I stuffed under the bed.

We were back in Vancouver in time for dinner. Fake Christmas had lasted just over twenty-four hours.

— 2 —

"Wash much?"

I sighed. Thing One (otherwise known as Ashley Anderson) stood by my desk, smirking down at me, flanked by Thing Two (otherwise known as Lauren Janicki).

"Shut your mouth much?" Phoebe snapped at her from the seat in front of me, like the awesome best friend she was.

"Honestly, some people could care less what they look like," Ashley said to Lauren.

"Couldn't," I said.

"What?"

"*Couldn't* care less. If you *could* care less, it means you could. Care less." Yeah. I really said that. Honestly, there are times when I wish I could tear out my own vocal cords.

Ashley's big eyes got a little bigger. "Oh. My. God. You are *such* a geek!" Still smirking, she strutted away, followed obediently by her posse of one.

Ashley was at the top of the food chain at Emily Carr Elementary. It didn't mean she was the most popular. It just meant she acted like she owned the place, and for some reason, we all went along with it. She radiated confidence, with her long chestnut brown hair, blue eyes, actual boobs, and unique sense of style. Like today, she was wearing hot pink tights, a long white T-shirt cinched at the waist with a big belt, black boots, big hoop earrings, and blue glitter eye shadow. On someone else, for example, *me,* it would've looked ridiculous. On Ashley, it looked cutting edge. Lauren was a copycat version of Ashley, only shorter and a bit odd-looking, like all her features were squished a little too close together.

Phoebe and I were a lot farther down the seventh-grade food chain. We weren't at the very bottom; we weren't like plankton, thank you very much. We were more like gazelles, or maybe field mice, which meant Thing One and Thing Two could eat us for breakfast whenever they felt like it.

I glanced down at my T-shirt. Sure enough, there was a food stain, most likely spaghetti sauce. I couldn't believe I hadn't noticed it this morning. Truth is, I'd been dressing Rosie and me in our least dirty dirty clothes since we got back from L.A. because the washing machine was still broken and Mom and I hadn't had a chance to get to the Laundromat yet.

I subtly dipped my head close to one pit, then the other, to do a B.O. check. Thank God all I could smell was deodorant.

"Do a couple of loads at my house later tonight," Phoebe whispered to me. "Cathy and Günter won't mind." Cathy and Günter are Phoebe's parents. Cathy is Chinese-Canadian and Günter is Swiss-Canadian. They're both psychologists, and neither of them like being called Mom and Dad because it sounds "too hierarchical."

"I think I'll take you up on that," I said to her. I held out my fist, and we did the Obama bump.

Phoebe had been my best friend since kindergarten, when the teacher made us bathroom buddies. Once I didn't make it in time and I peed my pants. Phoebe helped me flush my soaking underwear down the toilet and never breathed a word to anyone – even after the toilet backed up and flooded the basement and the school tried to find out who'd clogged the drain with a pair of Elmo briefs.

Now that's loyalty.

Phoebe also understood me better than anyone else, even my mom. Predictably, Mom flipped out over the Turd Incident. I'd been grounded for the rest of the

Christmas holidays, including New Year's Eve, which truly sucked since I had to turn down a whole bunch of party invitations – not. My mom never clued in that grounding me was pretty much a pointless punishment, since aside from hanging out with Phoebe – which I was still allowed to do, even when I was grounded – I had no social life.

But when I told Phoebe what had happened, this was what she said: "Wow." Then, "*How* big were they?" Then, "I can't believe they actually . . ." Then, "I get that you were tempted. But I can't believe you actually *did* it." And, finally, "You took out your anger on the wrong people."

Then we'd dropped the subject and exchanged Christmas gifts. I gave Phoebe a notebook with a stick figure of a boy on the cover that said *Boys Stink. Throw Rocks at Them.* She gave me a Magic 8 Ball. It was as big as a baseball, and it could supposedly predict the future. You could ask a question, give the ball a shake, and an answer would appear, floating on a little triangle, in a small round window at the base of the ball. We asked it a lot of questions, including my favorite: "Will Ashley's hair fall out in clumps this year?" The Magic 8 Ball responded, *It is certain.*

It was an awesome gift.

"Violet, look," Phoebe whispered. "It's your boyfriend."

Jean-Paul Bouchard had just entered the room. He'd arrived at our school in late October, from Winnipeg. He was seriously cute, but he was just as seriously *not* my boyfriend. One, because a guy like him would never even look at a girl like me, and two, because I had made a vow to myself post-Jonathan that I would never have a boyfriend because love is more trouble than it's worth.

We watched as Ashley subtly followed Jean-Paul's movements through the classroom, like a hunter tracking its prey. She was talking to Lauren and Claudia and doing a good job of acting like she was giving them her full attention. But the moment Jean-Paul sat down, Ashley broke away from her friends and slipped into the seat in front of him. She turned around, flashed him a pearly white smile, and started chatting.

"I hate her," I murmured.

"I want to be her," Phoebe replied.

And the two of us knew that it was perfectly natural to have both those feelings all at once.

Phoebe had a Mandarin lesson after school, so I picked up Rosie from her after-school care program in the basement on my own. When I came in, she was sitting in a corner, sucking her thumb.

"What's wrong, Rosie?"

"Isabelle tore my fairy wings." She took her thumb out of her mouth and held out the wings from the costume Dad had given her. One of them had a small tear. "She did it on purpose."

"Are you sure?"

"Yes."

"So why are you sitting in the corner?"

"Because I bit her."

"Oh."

Alison, one of the daycare workers, joined us. "It's the third time she's bitten Isabelle this year," she said to me, like Rosie wasn't there.

"The girl tore her wings. They were a present from our dad."

"That's still no excuse for biting. Will you tell your mother what happened, or should I write a note?"

I held out my hands and pulled Rosie to her feet, refusing to make eye contact with Alison. "I'll tell her," I lied. Then to Rosie, "I might be able to fix your wings."

I held Rosie's hand as we walked the two blocks to Main Street, my backpack slung over one shoulder, her backpack slung over the other. The hoods of our jackets were pulled up to protect us from the cold January rain.

When we reached Main Street, we stopped so Rosie could press her nose against the window of the Liberty

Bakery and gaze at the mouthwatering baked goods on display in the glass cases. A few blocks later, we crossed King Edward and stopped to inhale the aroma of bacon wafting from Helen's Diner. Another block up, we arrived outside the William Berto School of Hair Design. I opened the door, and we clomped up the stairs.

The school took up the entire second floor of the building. By the windows facing the street, a row of stations were set up for the students, with swivel chairs and giant mirrors. On the far wall was a row of sinks. A few students were at their stations, cutting and coloring customers' hair. Because they always needed heads to practice on, the school advertised five-dollar haircuts, and they got a steady stream of walk-ins.

"Girls, hi!" my mom said, waving us over. She was giving her friend Amanda a trim. She stopped what she was doing to give us each a hug.

Even though she was in her late thirties, my mom was still super-pretty. She had thick brown hair that fell just past her shoulders, green eyes, and lips that my dad used to call irresistibly kissable. She'd even managed to keep her figure, for the most part.

It was her clothes I couldn't stand. She'd started dressing differently after the divorce papers were signed. Her jeans were too tight, and her shirt was cropped to let her stomach show, a stomach that had had to stretch not once but twice to hold babies. A soft layer of flab drooped over the waist of her pants. To top it off, her belly button was pierced – a belated birthday gift from her friend Karen after they'd had a few too many margaritas one night.

I sat down in the chair next to Amanda's. "Good to see you guys," Amanda said, giving us each a high five. Amanda was younger than my mom and wore really cool clothes, a combination of secondhand stuff and amazing sweaters she'd knit herself. But even though she probably could have pulled it off, she didn't expose a lot of flesh. If only Mom had taken her fashion cues from Amanda and not her other best friend.

"Thanks for the hats; we wear them all the time," I said to Amanda as I took off my toque. She'd knit one for me and one for Rosie for Christmas. Mine was a dog hat, complete with eyes and whiskers, and the flaps on the sides were knit to look like beagle ears. Rosie's was a kitten hat, with little cat ears sewn onto the top.

"Can you cut my hair when you're done?" I asked my mom.

"I thought you were letting it grow out."

"I changed my mind."

"I wanna play in a chair," Rosie said. She loved to spin around and around in one of the chairs until she was so dizzy, she couldn't stand up.

"Sure thing, sweetie. Take the one in the far corner." Rosie skipped away.

Once she was gone, Amanda grabbed my hand and gave it a squeeze. "Violet, you know I love you. But cat turds?"

I turned to Mom. "Did you have to tell everyone?"

"Amanda isn't everyone," Mom replied. "She's one of my best friends."

"As long as you didn't tell your *other* best friend," I said, just as I heard a cackle behind me.

I didn't need to turn around because I could see her in the mirror: Karen, approaching at high speed. You know those old cartoons where the character has an angel version of himself sitting on one shoulder and a devil version on the other? Well, Amanda was like my mom's angel version because she brought out the best in her. Karen was like my mom's devil version because she brought out the worst.

"Cat turds!" She laughed, an unlit cigarette dangling from her mouth. "I've gotta hand it to you, Violet, that's a new low."

"Hey, Karen. Nice shirt," I said, nodding at her two-sizes-too-small sheer black top that announced, in big gold letters, *COUGAR*. I could clearly see her pink bra underneath. She wore a thick layer of makeup, and her hair was dyed platinum blonde.

Mom and Karen had what my mom referred to as "history." They used to work as a team in the film and TV business – Mom as the key hairstylist, Karen as her assistant. Karen was even there when my mom met my dad. Shortly after Rosie was born, Mom left the business to stay home with us, but when Dad took off, she needed to find a job fast. A job with regular hours and a steady paycheck. That's how she wound up teaching at the William Berto School of Hair Design. It was in the neighborhood, the pay was okay, and they loved my mom's work. Within a year, she was promoted to assistant manager. Six months later, Mom hired Karen, after she was fired from two productions in a row for showing up late all the time.

Yup. That was my mom in a nutshell: always wanting to see the best in people, even when it was clear to everyone else that they were nothing but losers.

"Maybe you need to see that therapist again," Karen said to me as she reapplied her lipstick in the mirror. "That's pretty twisted behavior."

My cheeks burned. Oh, how I hated her sometimes.

"Karen," my mom said in her warning voice, "I've dealt with it. And Violet's going to properly apologize, aren't you, Violet?"

"We really need to get the washing machine fixed," I said.

"I know. And we will, in a couple more weeks. I'm still paying off Christmas."

"If you could've seen Dad's new house –"

"Violet –"

"What about his new house?" asked Amanda.

"It's huge. They just bought it. Dad's obviously loaded. He has way more money than when you guys first split up."

"Violet, enough. We've been through this. I don't want to take more of his money."

"But *why*?"

"Because she doesn't want to get handouts from that cheating son of a bitch, right, Ingrid?" Karen said.

"Karen, do *not* trash-talk the girls' father in front of them," Mom said.

"Oops," Karen replied, not sounding the least bit apologetic. "I'm going out for a smoke." She tottered away in her platform wedgies. Amanda raised a discreet eyebrow at me in the mirror, and I raised one back. I was pretty sure Amanda wasn't nuts about Karen, either.

"I'm going to have to ask you to get supper for you and Rosie tonight," Mom said, as she turned her attention back to trimming Amanda's long red hair. "There's a pizza in the freezer."

"Why, what are you doing?" I asked, dreading the answer.

"I have a date."

Amazing how four little words can make you feel like you want to barf.

"Please tell us you're not going out with Alphonse again," said Amanda, wrinkling her nose.

Alphonse was this creep my mom had met on Havalife, an online dating service that Karen had convinced her to join. He was about the fifth guy she'd met that way. They'd all been losers, but Alphonse was in a category all his own. Twice, he'd taken my mom out to really fancy restaurants. Twice, he'd ordered the most expensive things on the menu. Twice, he'd "forgotten" his wallet and Mom had to pay.

"No, not Alphonse, give me some credit."

Amanda and I shared another look. We wanted to give her some credit, we really did.

"This is a new one. And I didn't meet him online. I met him in the flesh."

"Where?" asked Amanda.

"He came in for a haircut last week."

"So we know he's cheap," I said.

Mom ignored this. "He seems really sweet."

Which is exactly what you've said about all the other losers you've dated, I wanted to say.

"Really . . . genuine."

Ditto.

Amanda pursed her lips. But all she said was "Too bad we couldn't set you up with *him.*" She nodded at an eight-by-ten glossy photo that hung over Mom's workstation, beside a bunch of photos of Rosie and me. Smiling out at us from the picture was George Clooney.

Mom loved George Clooney. She'd loved him long before he'd become super-famous. Mom loved him from the first time she'd seen him in a sitcom called *The Facts of Life,* which was on TV when she was a teenager, back in the Dark Ages. I'd seen it a few times myself, on one of those cable channels that airs nothing but sitcoms from the 1980s, which seems to be a decade where everyone – even George – had really bad hair.

The photo my mom had was older than me, but it was personally signed to her because she'd actually *met* George Clooney. When she was still new to the business, she'd do what were known as day calls, filling in for stylists who were sick. One day, she'd been called to a movie set, and who walked into the trailer but George himself. She actually got to do his hair. That's right, she touched his head. And he obviously liked her because he'd written on the picture *To Ingrid – May Our Paths Cross Again.*

Even now, as she gazed at the photo, her expression went all mooshy. "He was amazing. So sweet, so charming. So freaking *gorgeous* . . . he was perfect."

"I wanted one pink streak! *One!*"

Mom tore her gaze away from George Clooney. Three stations away, an older woman was shrieking at a cowering male student. Every hair on her head was hot pink.

Mom took a deep breath. "I'll have to cut your hair another time, Violet." She put down her scissors and walked away to deal with the crisis.

I said good-bye to Amanda and collected Rosie from her chair. She wobbled and fell in a heap of giggles onto the floor. "That was fun!"

"C'mon," I said, pulling her to her feet and adjusting her glasses, which were crooked from all the spinning. "We have lots to do when we get home."

And I wasn't just talking about doing the laundry, finishing my homework, and making supper.

Because when Mom has a date, she isn't the only one who has to prepare for it.

— 3 —

He sat parked across the street in a banana yellow Toyota Corolla. Not a new model. I couldn't get a clear picture of him through my binoculars.

I was kneeling on my red beanbag chair, peering out the small dormer window between my bed and Rosie's. With my free hand, I dug into a box of Life cereal – a pre-pizza snack.

Suddenly Rosie came tearing into the bedroom, wearing nothing but her underpants. A colander was perched on her head. "Lemme see, lemme see!" She started jumping on her bed, careful not to hit her head on the sloped ceiling, then she launched herself onto the beanbag chair and tried to yank open the curtains.

"Rosie! You almost blew my cover," I scolded, as she

tried to grab the binoculars away from me. "Cut it out! He's opening his door."

I glanced at my watch. It was exactly 6:00 p.m. This put him a step ahead of Larry the Unibrow, who, during the brief period he'd dated my mom, showed up anywhere from half an hour to ninety minutes late. Of course, this made a lot more sense when Mom found out he was married. With four kids.

I tried to get a good look at her new date as he crossed the street, but he glanced up toward the window and I had to duck out of sight.

We listened as his feet thumped up the old wooden stairs. Then he rang the bell. We knew he'd rung the bell, even though we didn't hear it. It had been broken for over a year.

Rosie stood up, but I gripped her arm. "Rosie, you know the rules. Not yet. Besides, if you want to go to the door, you have to put on some clothes."

Rosie slipped on the clothes she'd been wearing earlier while I grabbed my Magic 8 Ball from its perch on my bookshelf.

I knew Mom's date was ringing the doorbell again. I knew he was starting to worry that he had the wrong address, or, worse, that he was being stood up.

"Will this guy be any better than all the others?" I asked the Magic 8 Ball, giving it a good shake and flipping it over.

Highly doubtful, it read. I placed it back on my bookshelf.

Finally – like I knew he would – he knocked.

"Violet, can you get that? I'm still putting on my face," my mom hollered from the bathroom down the hall.

"Got it," I shouted back.

"And be nice!"

I slowly made my way to the stairs. Rosie, the colander still on her head, tried to scoot around me, but I spread my arms to block her path.

"Lemme answer!" she shouted.

"Rosie. What have I told you?"

Rosie sighed. "Play it cool."

As we continued our leisurely descent, I said my little prayer: *Dear God, or Allah, or Buddha or Zeus or Whoever-You-Are, please let this one be okay. Please don't let him be a cheater (Jonathan), a cheapskate (Alphonse), an alcoholic (Carl), a creep (Guy), married (Larry), or a general, all-around jerk (Dimitri, Paulo, Jake, Yuri).*

I said this prayer even though I'm a cynic when it comes to love because I know that my mother is not. You'd think, after what had happened with Dad, that she'd have given up on men and found contentment in a life dedicated to child-rearing, hard work, and celibacy. But, no. Despite a growing list of epic failures, she had this freakish need to have a man in her life. So she dated like there was no tomorrow, always hoping the next guy would be The One.

Did I think this was a kind of sickness? Yes! *Did I find it tragic?* Of course! But I also knew that she wasn't going to stop until she'd found her version of The One, and that once she found him, Rosie and I were going to have to live with it too because, let's face it, we were a package deal.

So, yeah – a small part of me had no choice but to hope that the next guy would be so spectacularly awesome, he'd put an end to the serial dating that was torture for all of us.

Just as he started to knock again, I opened the door.

The guy blinked like a startled mole. "Oh, hi. I was beginning to think no one was home."

I gave him my classic once-over.

He was pudgy. His pale skin was sprinkled with freckles. His ears were too small for his head. His hair was reddish brown and thinning. He was wearing a loud multicolored sweater. Its loose fit did not manage to hide his man-boobs.

"You must be Rosie," he said, bending down to shake her hand. "I like your hat."

Rosie beamed up at him. "It's a crown."

I love my little sister. I really do. But she made my job very difficult because, like Mom, she's an optimist, which means she likes *all* of Mom's dates, at least in the beginning.

"And you must be Violet," he said to me, holding out his hand. I shook it. His skin was moist and clammy. "I'm Dudley," he continued. "Dudley Wiener."

Groan. I'd seen enough. I turned away without another word. I walked back up the stairs and into our bedroom, where I threw our clothes and sheets into a laundry bag to take to Phoebe's house. Then I went into Mom's room and added her clothes to the bag. When I was done, I lined up all the makeup and perfume on her dresser in precise little lines, tallest to shortest.

This was the tenth guy my mom had dated post-Dad. The tenth guy who wouldn't be good enough for her. The tenth guy who'd either dump her because she was too clingy, or who'd do something so awful, she'd be forced to dump him. The tenth guy who wouldn't come close to being The One.

I couldn't be a bystander any longer. Something had to be done.

— 4 —

But first, a little history.

My mom and dad met fourteen years ago, on the set of a TV show called *Crime Beaters*. It was about a bunch of homicide cops who solved a different murder each week. My dad was the first assistant director, which means he shouted at the crew to hurry up and shoot scenes before they lost their light, or their time, or their money. My mom was the on-set hair person, which means she combed and sprayed and bobby-pinned the actors' and actresses' hair in between takes. One day, by accident, she blasted some hair spray right into my dad's eyes. He started to curse. Mom poured water into his eyes and leaned in really close to him, her big green eyes full of concern. According to my dad, "That's when I knew I was going to marry this woman."

They tied the knot a year later. Three months after that, I was born. You can do the math.

When I was five years old, they bought the house just east of Main Street. It was a "heritage" home, which Dad said was just a fancy word for "falling apart." But he was good with his hands, Mom had a great eye for cheap but cool-looking furniture, and together they turned the house into a home. Mom still worked on occasional shoots when she could find good child care for me, and Dad started getting directing gigs, first on *Crime Beaters,* then on other TV series. When I was almost seven, Rosie was born, and Mom and Dad decided that Mom would put work on hold for a few years.

Two years later, when I was nine going on ten, Dad got a job directing a bunch of episodes for a TV series called *Paranormal Pam.* It was about a woman who investigated ghost sightings. The twist was that she was a ghost herself.

I remember sitting at dinner with Dad on the weekends (the only time we ate meals with him while he was directing because he worked really long hours), and he would say things like "I think this show is going to be a hit. The star – Jennica Valentine – is a real find. . . .

"Jennica is unbelievably talented. I had my doubts at first – I just figured she was another blonde bimbo – but, no, she's got substance. And she's only twenty-four. . . .

"Jennica said the funniest thing today. . . ."

I guess you could say the clues were there.

One day, Mom decided to surprise Dad by taking us all to the set, so we could have lunch with him. At first, it was sort of like a homecoming for her. Even though Mom had never worked on *Paranormal Pam,* she knew a lot of the crew. Including Karen.

"Ingrid! It's about frigging time you came to visit!" Karen said, when we entered the hair and makeup trailer. She put me into her chair and started braiding my hair, and, even though I could smell her stale cigarette breath, it was kind of nice.

"I hope Ian's treating you well," my mom said.

I was gazing into the mirror, and I saw a look pass between Karen and one of the makeup artists.

"It's not the same without you here," Karen replied.

After Karen finished braiding my hair, Mom took us to find Dad. They'd just broken for lunch, but Dad wasn't in the lunch tent, and no one answered when we knocked on his trailer door.

We were still standing there when another trailer door opened nearby and a woman with long blonde hair, big boobs, and tons of makeup stepped out.

Followed by my dad, who was buckling his belt.

You know that expression "the color drained from his face"? That's what happened to my dad when he spotted us.

So I might have been only nine, but I knew something big was going down. I didn't know what, exactly, but I did know that a man shouldn't be buckling his belt in front of a woman who wasn't his wife.

"Ingrid, hi!" Dad said, forcing a smile. "What a nice surprise."

"We thought we'd join you for lunch," Mom said, her voice a weird monotone. "But I can see you're busy."

"No, no, Jennica and I were just going over some line changes, that's all. Jennica, this is Ingrid, my, *um,* wife."

Jennica's face turned fire engine red. "Hi, there! I've heard so much about you."

"And these are my girls, Violet and Rose," Dad continued, trying to act like everything was perfectly normal.

"What lovely names! I love violets," she said to me.

I hid behind my mom.

Jennica's smile was frozen on her face. "Well, nice to meet you," she said, then ducked back into her trailer and slammed the door.

Dad turned to us and smiled. "Well, troops, shall we eat?"

"Screw you, Ian," my mom said quietly. "You will tell me everything when you get home." Clutching Rosie to her chest, she grabbed my hand, pulling me so hard I thought my arm would come out of its socket. Dad didn't try to stop her.

That night, Mom got what she asked for.

He told her everything.

"Your mother and I are going to live apart for a while," Dad announced a week later. He'd taken me on a bike ride to La Casa Gelato. We were sitting outside, and I was working my way through a massive cone of Rocky Road. (Phoebe told me later that my choice of flavors was psychologically significant. Her parents' profession couldn't help but rub off on her somewhat.)

"Why?" I asked.

"It has nothing to do with you, sweetie. It's just that sometimes adults . . . they fall out of love."

"You've fallen out of love with Mommy?"

"Not exactly. I still love her. I always will, in a way."

"But you love the blonde lady with the boobs better."

There was a pause. "Jennica. Her name is Jennica."

Two weeks later, Dad moved out of our house and into a furnished apartment in Yaletown. Rosie and I slept over on Wednesdays and every other weekend. This change in our routine didn't seem to bother Rosie at first; she was only two, and she acted like the whole thing was just a temporary adventure.

As for me, I was having trouble sleeping. I couldn't help thinking about what had gone on *before* Dad buckled his belt, when he and Jennica were alone in the trailer.

As Phoebe said, it was a lot for a kid to process.

Luckily Jennica was never over at his apartment when we were there. But sometimes Dad would plop us in front of the TV and go into his bedroom and close the door and have long talks with her on the phone.

Once, when he was talking to her, I picked up one of his *Paranormal Pam* scripts, which he'd left lying on the glass-topped coffee table. I randomly flipped it open to a page and read.

```
INT. JOE'S HOUSE - LIVING ROOM - NIGHT
PAM is talking to JOE, a 40-year-old client.
They are both gazing at the ghost of a
BEAUTIFUL WOMAN dressed in 1920s-style
clothes, standing by his mantelpiece.

                    JOE
        I keep seeing her hovering
        there.
```

PAM

Does your wife see her?

JOE

Never.

Pam considers this.

PAM

You know, Joe, a woman did die in this house, in 1927.

JOE

How?

PAM

She died of a broken heart. She loved her husband madly, but he was having an affair. One morning, she just didn't wake up.

She looks at Joe, hard.

PAM

Are you cheating on your wife, Joe?

```
Joe doesn't answer, but looks away guiltily.

                    PAM
     I suspect only you can see the
     ghost because of your guilty
     conscience. She's trying to
     tell you that an affair can
     cause unbelievable heartache.
     Do you want to destroy your
     marriage? Do you?
```

I could hear Dad in the other room, still talking quietly to Jennica. Rosie was staring at the TV, transfixed. I picked my nose, smeared the booger on the page I'd just read, and closed the script.

Phoebe would later tell me that this was classic passive-aggressive behavior.

Whatever. I just knew that, in the moment, it felt pretty good.

At our place, my mom was trying hard not to fall apart. Most nights, Karen or Amanda would come over with a pizza or a frozen lasagna for dinner, and once Rosie and I had gone to bed, they'd talk long into the night. I was glad my mom had her girlfriends because the mood around the house during those first few months pretty much sucked. At least when Karen and Amanda were over, I could escape to Phoebe's house without feeling guilty.

"We can't just sit here and let this happen," Phoebe said to me one weekend, while we were holed up in my room. She'd stayed for dinner and witnessed my mom crying over the kitchen sink as she washed the dishes.

"But what can we do?" I asked.

Phoebe thought for a moment. "I saw this movie with my parents once. Some crazy woman was in love with this guy, but he was in love with someone else. So she made a voodoo doll of his fiancée and started to make the fiancée sick with black magic. It gave me nightmares for months." Cathy and Günter took Phoebe to all sorts of movies that were what my mom called "age-inappropriate."

"Are you suggesting we make a voodoo doll of Jennica?"

"Precisely. Then we can put a curse on her. Not to kill her, of course. Just to get her away from your dad."

Phoebe was an excellent ideas person.

So we printed some instructions from the web and got to work. Using scraps of fabric and stuffing, we made a basic doll, about six inches high. When the body of the doll was complete, Phoebe stitched a mouth onto it, and I sewed on two buttons for eyes.

"We need hair," Phoebe said. "Jennica's hair. And we need a personal object that belongs to her."

The next time I was over at Dad's, I snuck into his bedroom while he was cooking dinner. It didn't take me long to find a lipstick that had rolled under the bed. In the bathroom I found a pink hairbrush, filled with long blonde hairs. I pulled the hairs out of the brush and slipped them into a Baggie, along with the lipstick.

After school the next day, Phoebe and I went to her house. We stuck the hair on the doll's head with some glue, then smeared Jennica's lipstick on its mouth. We held the doll up to the light, feeling quite proud of our work.

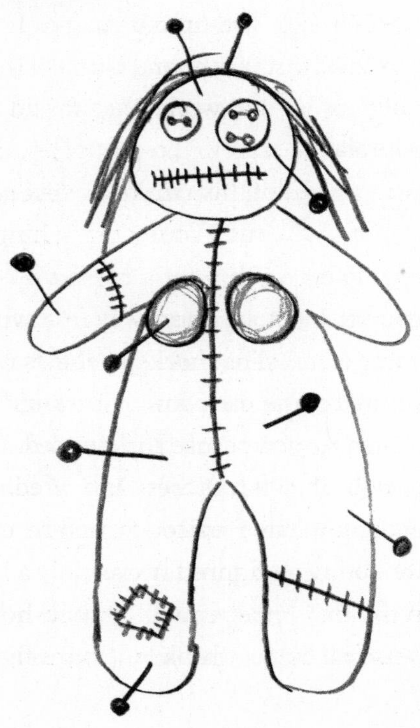

Then we cast the spell. We stuck a bunch of straight pins into the Jennica doll and chanted, "May ill fortune befall you! May you be forced to leave this city! May you leave Ian's life forever!" We repeated this process every day for a month.

On the final day, Karen dropped by to see Mom. Phoebe and I were in the kitchen doing homework.

"Ingrid, I have some interesting news," Karen announced, as she pulled out a bottle of wine. "Violet, Phoebe. Am-scray."

We clomped down the stairs to the basement and turned on the TV. Then we tiptoed back up the stairs and listened at the basement door.

"The show wrapped last week," Karen said. "Jennica took the first plane back to Los Angeles. Said she couldn't wait to get out of this rain-drenched town."

"Really," Mom said, and I could hear a hint of hopefulness creep into her voice.

"And they screened an episode at the wrap party. What a steaming turd. I'd be shocked if it gets renewed."

Phoebe and I tiptoed back down the stairs and did a little dance, convinced our curse had worked.

Sure enough, just like Karen had predicted, the network aired only three episodes before canceling the show. Phoebe and I figured it was only a matter of time before my dad came crawling back home with his tail between his legs. I think my mom figured the same thing because she started taking showers again.

So we were all blindsided when Dad announced that he was moving to L.A. to live with Jennica.

And that he was filing for divorce.

And that Jennica was pregnant with the twins.

That night, my sister wet her bed for the first time. After she fell back to sleep, I took all of my books off the shelf and carefully rearranged them in alphabetical order by author, from Louisa May Alcott to Paul Zindel.

When I was done, I took them all down again and rearranged them in alphabetical order by title, from *Are You There God? It's Me, Margaret* to *Wind in the Willows.*

It was the first time I'd ever done a weirdly obsessive thing like that. But it wouldn't be the last.

— 5 —

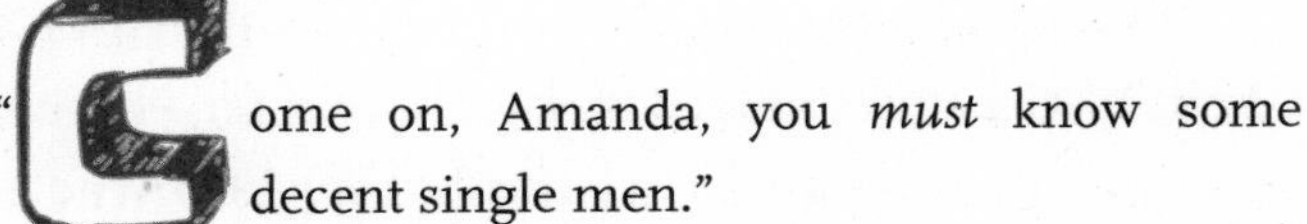

“Come on, Amanda, you *must* know some decent single men.”

It was a rainy Saturday morning, and Phoebe and I were talking to Amanda in the knitting shop she owned on Main Street. It was called Wild and Woolly and was just a couple of blocks away from the William Berto School of Hair Design. Mom and Amanda had met when Mom signed up for Amanda’s first-ever “Stitch and Bitch” workshop five years ago. As far as I could tell, this meant a group of women got together in her store after hours and did ten percent knitting, thirty percent drinking, and sixty percent complaining about men. They’d been good friends ever since.

“If I did, don’t you think I’d have introduced them to your mom by now?” Amanda answered, as she stocked a shelf with balls of emerald green angora wool. "Besides, your mom tells me this new guy is different."

"She said that about Paulo, too," Phoebe said.

"And Jonathan, and Alphonse, and Guy," I added.

Amanda sighed. "Yeah, I know. But maybe she's right this time."

"Please. I've met him. He looks like Mole Man."

"Who's Mole Man?"

"I don't know, I made it up. But that's what he looks like – part man, part mole."

"And his name is Dudley *Wiener,*" Phoebe added.

"Now, girls. Don't judge a book by its cover," Amanda said, as she headed back to the counter, Phoebe and I trailing behind her. "Remember, my boyfriend's name is Cosmo."

"True," I replied, "but Cosmo is hot."

"Totally," sighed Phoebe.

Confession: I might be a love cynic, but Amanda and Cosmo were the one couple I rooted for. They'd been seeing each other for almost two years and were perfect for each other, like a right shoe and a left. When I saw them together, my heart did like the Grinch's when he heard little Cindy Lou Who sing that day . . . it grew.

"Cosmo must have some friends," I said.

But Amanda just laughed as she tucked a piece of her long red hair behind her ear. "He has plenty of friends. And I wouldn't wish any of them on your mother."

"They couldn't be any worse than Guy. Or that drunk Karen set her up with," said Phoebe.

"Carl," I said.

"True," Amanda replied. "But they're still not good enough for your mom. Besides, it's not all about looks and names, and you know it. Maybe Dudley's got a great personality."

"Highly doubtful," I said. "But I guess I'll find out tonight."

"Tonight?" Amanda raised an eyebrow.

"She's invited him to dinner."

"Wow. That was fast."

I nodded glumly. Usually we were spared that unique form of torture until after she'd had at least a few dates. And since Mom hadn't even mentioned her first date with Dudley afterward, I kind of figured it was over before it had ever really started.

Last night, I found out I was wrong.

What happened was this: Mom arrived home shortly after six, carrying a DVD and a take-out bag full of Thai food from Sawasdee, just like she did every Friday night. Rosie placed a blanket in front of the TV, and I arranged the food on top of the blanket while Mom grabbed a cold beer for herself and glasses of milk for Rosie and me. Then Mom popped in the movie, and we all sat down on the blanket and started to eat.

It was the same routine week after week, and I loved it. See, Friday night is the official Gustafson Girls' Night. It's the one night of the week that Mom keeps free and clear for me and Rosie. No dates, no company – not even Phoebe or Karen or Amanda. Just the three of us.

Anyway, last night we were about half an hour into *Ocean's Eleven*, a caper movie starring George Clooney, when the phone rang. We aren't supposed to answer the phone during Gustafson Girls' Night. But when Mom saw the number on call display, she picked up, blatantly breaking one of our rules.

"Hello?" Mom said, like she didn't already know who it was. "Dudley, hi . . ." She left the room, clutching the portable phone to her ear. She was gone for almost half an hour. I know because Rosie and I watched a whole episode of "Jeopardy!" while we waited.

When she returned, I said, "You do realize you are in violation of a number of official Gustafson Girls' Night rules."

"Sorry," she said, not sounding sorry at all. "I hope you girls don't mind . . . I've invited Dudley to dinner tomorrow night."

"What? You've only been on one date," I protested.

"Well, yes and no. We've had coffee every morning this week."

"Really." It bugged me that I hadn't known this. "What kind of job does he have that he has time to sit around drinking coffee with you every morning?" I asked. "Or is he 'between jobs' like Jake?"

"He owns a bath shop. It doesn't open till ten."

"A bath shop. Like, he sells tubs?"

"No, items for the bath. Towels, shower curtains, soap dishes –"

"Toilets?"

"No, Violet."

"Toilets for pooping in," giggled Rosie.

"Anyway," Mom continued, "he'd like to meet you both."

"Why? Is he a pedophile?"

"Violet!"

I was getting on her nerves, and it felt quite satisfying.

"What's a pedal file?" asked Rosie.

At that point, Mom just grabbed the remote and restarted the movie, and that had been the end of that.

"You're *sure* Cosmo doesn't have any friends?" I asked Amanda again.

"For the last time, I'm sure. And might I point out, it's not really your job to find a man for your mom."

"I couldn't agree more," I said. "But since she's so dead-set on having a man in her life, and since her choices affect us, too –"

"Yeah, remember the rock-throwing incident?" Phoebe interjected.

"I've made it my mission to find someone more suitable," I concluded.

"And I'm her sidekick," Phoebe said. "The Watson to her Sherlock. The Gayle to her Oprah. The Robin to her Batman –"

"I get it," Amanda said. "So you don't think Dudley's The One?"

"God, no."

"I think Dudley's nice," Rosie announced as she joined us from the back of the store, where she'd been checking out the bins of buttons.

"You think everyone's nice," I reminded her. "And you met him for five minutes."

"He liked my crown," she said, like that was somehow significant.

The bell jingled over the door to the shop and Cosmo entered, followed by a couple of customers. "Hey, girls," Cosmo said when he saw us. "Hey, gorgeous," he said to Amanda. When his eyes met hers, his expression went all soft and goopy. Then he took her hand and kissed her fingers one by one, and she smiled, and it was like they were the only two people in the world. I could feel my heart expanding.

"We'll go," I said.

"Bye, girls. Go turn some heads," Cosmo said. And even though we knew it was just Cosmo being Cosmo, Phoebe and I both giggled like a couple of dorks.

Amanda walked us to the door. "Violet?" she said. "Give Dudley a chance tonight, okay? Don't get up to your old tricks."

"What old tricks?" I asked innocently as we stepped outside.

The three of us walked a couple of blocks farther down Main Street to the Liberty Bakery. Mom had given us some money to buy ourselves a treat, like she did every Saturday, so that she could shop at Costco in peace. The sidewalks were slick with rain, and we had to dart our way in and out of a sea of umbrellas.

The bakery was bright and warm and smelled like yeast and sugar. I bought a Nanaimo bar, and Phoebe and Rosie got fudge brownies. We were just about to leave with our treats when a boy walked in. Phoebe grabbed my arm and pinched me, hard.

"Ow!" I said.

Then I saw what she saw. It wasn't just any boy, it was Jean-Paul. He was wearing jeans and a dripping-wet bomber jacket on his lanky frame, and his dark wavy hair was plastered to the sides of his head. It accentuated his nose, which was rather large.

"Oh my God," I murmured. "He's adorable."

"This from the girl who's vowed to never have a boyfriend," teased Phoebe, who took every opportunity to let me know that she thought my vow was ridiculous.

I shrugged. "It doesn't mean I can't appreciate the opposite sex on a purely aesthetic level."

He'd spotted us. "Hi, Phoebe. Hi, Violet," he said.

"Hi," Phoebe and I replied in unison. I tried to think of something more to say. "This is Rosie," I said, pointing at my sister.

"Hi, Rosie," he said. Then to me, "Nice shoes."

I was wearing my new Converse high tops with the skull and rose motif.

"Thanks."

"I'm just buying some bread for my mother," he said.

"Oh," I replied.

Silence.

"Well," Jean-Paul said eventually, "see you in school."

He was about to move past us into the lineup when I blurted, *"Parlez-vous français?"*

His face lit up. *"Oui, bien sûr, je parle français. Mon père vient de Québec. Et toi?"*

I stared at him blankly. *"Pamplemousse,"* I replied.

He looked at me like he was trying to figure out if I was making a joke. He must have decided I was because he gave a halfhearted laugh before he joined the lineup.

Phoebe, Rosie, and I stepped outside, pulling up the hoods on our rain jackets.

"Why did you call him a grapefruit?" Phoebe asked.

I groaned. "I thought I was saying 'fantastic.'"

"That's *fantastique*."

"Great. Now he thinks I'm an idiot. Or a French-hater."

"So? What do you care what he thinks of you?"

"I don't."

"Liar. Besides, I think he likes you. He spoke actual words to you!"

I rolled my eyes. I appreciated Phoebe's belief that a guy like Jean-Paul would even look twice at a scrawny and forgettable girl like me. But seriously. As if.

The three of us turned toward home. We came to Phoebe's house first. It was new, but designed to look like the other older homes in the neighborhood. Phoebe ran inside to tell her mom that she was heading to my place. A couple of minutes later, she came running out, clutching a Tupperware container.

"Günter's apple strudel," she said. I was pretty sure Phoebe's parents thought Rosie and I were undernourished because they were always sending Phoebe over to our house with large amounts of homemade food.

Eight houses down, we arrived at our place. It was painted *aubergine,* which is a fancy word for eggplant, which is a fancy word for purple. The paint was peeling. The grass was ankle-high. One of the gutters was broken and dangled over the front porch. The railing leading up the front steps wobbled dangerously. An old love seat that we'd meant to bring to the Salvation Army was still sitting on our porch a year later, its insides hanging out, torn up by a family of mice.

The neighbors were walking to their car. "Hi, Mr. and Mrs. Bright," I said, even though I was pretty sure they wouldn't respond. And they didn't; they just gave me the hairy eyeball.

The Brights used to talk to us, when my dad was around. They'd even given me a box of musty old books when they found out how much I like to read, and there were a few treasures in there, including an early edition of *Stuart Little* by E.B. White. But once

Dad left, Mom couldn't keep up with the home repairs. The Brights dropped subtle hints. Then not-so-subtle hints. Then, last year, they called city hall. We knew this because a man came around to our house to follow up on their complaint. He told us that the Brights had called our property "a disgrace to the neighborhood." Mom lit into the guy, telling him that she'd like to see *him* try to maintain an older home as a single parent raising two kids on a limited budget. He backed right off.

Inside, Phoebe, Rosie, and I peeled off our rain jackets and dumped them in a heap on the floor. Mom was still at Costco, so we sat at the kitchen table and devoured our Liberty Bakery treats and Günter's strudel all in one go. When we were done and I'd made Rosie have two glasses of milk because her bones were growing, I sent her to the basement to watch a video. That's right, a video. We had a DVD player in the living room, but Mom had bought the VCR at a yard sale for ten bucks, and since then she'd picked up hundreds of videos for as little as twenty-five cents because no one wanted them anymore.

"Okay," said Phoebe, belching softly. "Let's make a list of every single man we know."

I grabbed a pen and a pad of paper.

SINGLE MEN WE KNOW

by Violet G. and Phoebe S.

1) Mr. Patil, our teacher. Rumor has it he still lives in his parents' basement and spends all his money on his model train set.
2) Daryl, the guy who runs the local pet shop. Nice guy, but weighs about three hundred pounds and smells like gerbil poo.
3) Mohamed Karami, a student at Mom's hair design school. Handsome and hilarious; also gay.
4) Donald Somebody-or-other. Works with Phoebe's dad. Nice enough, but pretty ancient and supposedly has had both hips replaced.
5) Frank, the homeless guy. Sometimes hangs out on Main Street and writes poems on scraps of paper.

We both agreed it was a pathetic list. Finding a good man for my mom was clearly going to be a daunting task.

"Hi, Phoebe. Hi, Violet," Mom said as she lugged bags of groceries into the house.

"Hi, Ms. Gustafson," said Phoebe as she nonchalantly folded the list and slipped it into her pocket.

"Violet, I need you to help me bring the groceries in from the Rust Bucket." The Rust Bucket was the name she'd given to our '95 Mazda. "Then I need you and your sister to help me clean up the house. Dudley's supposed to be here in an hour, and I haven't even showered yet."

Phoebe got up. "I should get home, anyway. Cathy and Günter are taking me to a poetry slam tonight." Phoebe's parents were always introducing her to new cultural experiences.

I walked her to the door.

"Have you got your questions memorized for tonight?" she asked.

I tapped my head. "It's all up here."

"I wish I could watch."

"Me, too. But it's better if you don't. I might need you for down the road."

"Do you think there's going to be a *down the road*?"

I took a deep breath. "I seriously hope not."

— 6 —

Chew, chew, chew . . . chew, chew, chew . . . I could hear The Wiener masticating his food. There was a rhythm to it, like he was eating to a song that played inside his head. From where I sat on his immediate left, I could see right into his ear, which was full of yellow wax and little red hairs. It was enough to make me lose my appetite. To complete the package, he was wearing a white-and-blue striped button-up shirt with a green and red and black plaid sweater-vest on top.

Ugh.

The Wiener arrived just as Rosie and I finished cleaning the house. We'd had to hang up our coats and put away our shoes and take all our stray toys, books, homework, dolls, games, sweaters, and socks up to our bedroom. Then we'd thrown out all the granola bar wrappers, snot rags, and strands of dental floss that covered the coffee table in the living room. After that, Mom hauled out the vacuum cleaner and vacuumed the whole main floor – even under the couches, where the really big dust bunnies lived. I told Rosie I could hear them scream as they got sucked up, which made her cry, so Mom made me apologize. Then, while Rosie escaped to the basement, I had to help Mom wash all the dishes that had piled up during the week. Our house hadn't been this clean since she'd dated Jonathan.

The Wiener, *aka* Dudley, remembered to knock this time. And he'd brought a gift for the house. It was in a rectangular box, wrapped in pretty metallic paper. Rosie and I gazed at it hungrily, convinced it was chocolates.

"Go ahead and open it," he said, grinning.

Rosie tore apart the paper and opened the box. "What is it?" she asked, her nose wrinkling like she'd just smelled a bad fart.

"It's a soap dish," I told her.

"How thoughtful," Mom said as she appeared from upstairs, wearing too much makeup and a blouse that was too tight. "Pretty *and* practical."

I could tell from the look on Rosie's face that Dudley had just gone down a notch in her estimation. Which wasn't necessarily a bad thing.

—

"What a delicious meal," Dudley said as he polished off his second helping, smacking his lips. For a moment, I thought he might actually pick up the plate and lick it clean. "You're an excellent cook, Ingrid."

"Thank you," my mom replied. She'd made her famous roasted lemon chicken. I was tempted to point out that it was her *only* famous dish; that she rarely made home-cooked meals these days; that our family survived mainly on food of the heat 'n' serve variety – like pizza, chicken strips, lasagna, and fish sticks – because Mom was either too tired to cook after standing on her feet all day, or she had a date. But I had important work ahead of me, so I kept my mouth shut.

"When I cook for myself . . . well, *lettuce* just say I make a *hash* of it . . . and afterward, you never *sausage* a mess." Dudley smiled, waiting for us to laugh.

We didn't.

Well, Mom did a little, but I was pretty sure it was just to be polite.

"Are you Scottish?" I asked him.

"*Um,* twenty-five percent, yes. On my mother's side. Why?"

"Your sweater-vest. I thought maybe it was your clan tartan."

"Violet," said Mom in her warning voice.

"What? Andrew MacDonald, in my class? He did a presentation on his Scottish heritage and came to school wearing a kilt. He told us each clan had its own tartan."

"What's a tartan?" asked Rosie.

"It's an ugly plaid pattern," I told her. "Like that." I pointed at Dudley's vest.

"Violet!" my mom said again.

"It's okay." Dudley laughed. "I don't have a great deal of fashion sense. In fact, I got this at a yard sale for fifty cents."

"What a steal," Mom said, and she actually sounded impressed.

"I get a lot of my clothes at yard sales."

Gross.

"I love yard sales," Mom said.

"Really?"

"The plate you're eating from? Yard sale. The chair you're sitting on? Yard sale."

I couldn't believe it. My mother was bonding with Dudley over his supreme cheapness.

"Perhaps when spring rolls around," The Wiener continued, "we might visit a few sales together."

"I'd like that."

They beamed at each other.

"Let me get this straight," I said. "You get five-dollar haircuts and buy your clothes at yard sales. Are you *sure* you're not Scottish?"

"Violet!"

"What? Andrew MacDonald told us that while it's a stereotype, all stereotypes are based on an element of truth."

"Actually, I'm more Austrian than anything else," Dudley explained to me. He didn't seem remotely offended by my comments. "On my dad's side. My great-grandparents immigrated to Canada from Vienna. In Austrian, Vienna is spelled *W-I-E-N*. Hence my last name. It means 'someone from Vienna.' *Wiener.*"

"That must have sucked growing up," I said.

My mom put her head in her hands, but Dudley just laughed again. "It did. I got teased mercilessly. I actually thought about changing my last name, but I'm glad I didn't. Now I'm proud to be a Wiener."

I'd just taken a drink of milk, which sprayed out of my nose.

"Why don't we move into the living room for dessert?" Mom said, her voice a little high-pitched. She scraped back her chair so fast, it almost fell over. "Violet, you can help me clear the table."

"Actually, Rosie's volunteered to clear the table," I said, winking at Rosie, who was in on my plan. She tried to wink back, but since she didn't know how, it was more of a blink. "I'll keep Dudley company in the other room."

My mom's eyes narrowed. As I walked past her, she whispered to me, "Be kind."

"Of course," I said.

I didn't bother adding that sometimes you have to be cruel to be kind.

The Wiener settled onto our red couch. I sat across from him on our gold couch. He smiled. I didn't. I just stared at him without blinking. I was pretty good at it. He looked away after only a few seconds, like I knew he would.

I always won the stare-down.

He shifted in his seat, like he was trying to get comfortable. "So," he began, "you're in seventh grade, is that right –"

"Mom says you run a bathroom store," I said, cutting him off. I picked up a small notebook and pen from the side table, where I'd placed them before supper.

"A bath shop. That's right. It's at Main and Eleventh."

"Do you own it? Or do you just work there?"

"I own it," he said.

I wrote that down. "How long have you owned this business?"

"Four years."

"I see. And what did you do before then?"

He shifted in his seat again. "I was in the insurance business, selling household insurance, car insurance, you name it."

"Why did you leave? Were you fired?"

"No, I chose to leave. I got tired of working for a big faceless company. I decided to go into business for myself."

I nodded. "What do you earn in a year?"

Dudley squirmed again. He took a deep breath. "Let's put it this way, I do just fine."

"And yet you buy previously worn clothes at yard sales."

He smiled. "Your mom likes yard sales, too."

"My mom is a single parent raising two kids with very little support from my dad. What's your excuse?"

He shrugged. "I guess I love a bargain."

I wrote the word *CHEAP* in capital letters.

"Do you have any debt?" I continued.

"No."

"Mortgage?"

"No. I rent an apartment. I used to own a house – why am I telling you this?"

Just then Rosie dashed into the living room and plunked herself beside Dudley. She beamed up at him. "Hello," she said, adjusting her glasses.

"Hello," Dudley replied.

"Are you married?" I continued.

Dudley almost choked on his wine. "No, Violet. I am not married. I really think this has gone far enough –"

"We're almost finished. Are you an addict of any sort? Alcohol, drugs – illegal or prescription?"

Dudley took a deep breath. "I see what you're doing, and I think it's admirable. But these questions, they're awfully personal."

"So you do have an addiction."

"I didn't say that –"

"It's a simple question."

"No, I don't have any addictions. I'm a pretty normal guy, all in all." He squirmed in his seat again.

"Then why do you act like a man who's got something to hide?"

"What are you talking about?"

"You keep squirming."

Dudley stood up. He lifted the couch cushion and pulled something out. It was one of Rosie's dolls. "*That*'s why I'm squirming."

Rosie giggled. "I got tired of carrying everything upstairs, so I putted Roxanna under the cushion."

Dudley handed Rosie her doll. "Sorry to disappoint you, Violet. But there aren't any skeletons in my closet."

"Skeletons? Closet? What are you guys talking about?" Mom asked as she entered the room with dessert. She looked from me to Dudley, smiling anxiously.

The Wiener glanced at me. And I have to give the guy a bit of credit because he didn't rat me out. All he said was "Oh, just this and that. Violet has been keeping me quite entertained."

“What are they doing, what are they doing?” Rosie said, trying to squeeze in beside me. The Wiener had just left, and Mom was walking him to his car, which was pretty stupid since his Corolla was parked right across the street and our neighborhood was not exactly a hotbed of crime.

“They’re just talking,” I told Rosie. Then, because I was in a generous mood, I shoved over a bit so she could squeeze in beside me. Now we were both crouched down on our knees, peering out the living room window. The curtains were drawn on either side of us, leaving just the tiniest opening for our heads. The windowsill, which hadn’t been a part of our cleaning spree, was thick with a layer of dust, so I wrote my name in it to pass the time.

After what felt like an eternity’s worth of small talk, Dudley reached into his pocket for his car keys. His car was so old, he actually had to insert the key into the door to unlock it.

Maybe he got his car at a yard sale too, I thought, making myself laugh.

Dudley turned back to my mom and held out his arm, like he was about to shake her hand. Then, without warning, he lunged at her, planting his lips over her lips like a toilet plunger and awkwardly pulling her into an embrace.

I waited for Mom to push him away, maybe even slap him across the face like they did in the movies. But she didn’t. In fact, kind of the opposite. She threw her arms around *him,* too, and started kissing him back.

"Ew!" Rosie giggled, her thumb flying into her mouth. *"Ew!"*

This wasn't the first time post-divorce that I'd seen my mother making out with a man she'd practically just met. But as far as I knew, it *was* the first time the Brights had seen it. I saw them now, coming up the street with their little dog, Benjamin. I could tell they were trying not to look. But it was like passing a car accident. You know you might see something disturbing and gross, and yet you look anyway.

"Violet, why are you crying?" Rosie said to me, pulling her thumb out of her mouth to pat my hand.

I took my glasses off and wiped my eyes. "I'm fine," I said. "It must be allergies. Let's go to the basement and find a movie."

We traipsed downstairs. I found *Toy Story 2* among our huge assortment of videos and put it in the machine for Rosie. Then I pulled the rest of the videos off the shelf. Last time, I shelved them alphabetically by title. Tonight I arranged them alphabetically by star. *F. Murray Abraham, Ben Affleck, Kirstie Alley.* Whenever I came across a star whose last name was in the second half of the alphabet, I placed the video into a separate pile. *Bruce Willis, Patrick Swayze, Brad Pitt, Wedding.*

Wedding. My mom and dad gazed up at me from the cover, twelve years younger, cheeks touching, grinning smugly like they were in on their own little secret. A cheesy heart framed the picture. The video had been a wedding gift from one of Dad's friends, a cameraman who'd shot all kinds of footage of their happy day.

I threw it like a Frisbee across the room, and it skidded to a halt near the opposite wall. Then I continued rearranging the videos. *Jennifer Aniston, Alec Baldwin, Drew Barrymore.*

I loved my mom so much. And I hated my dad for turning her into a woman who'd let practically any guy kiss her because she was so desperate to find a replacement for him – someone who would love her the way he'd loved her, but for real this time.

Jeff Bridges, Gabriel Byrne, George Clooney.

She deserved a man far, far better than The Wiener, or The Cheater, or The Unibrow, or The Creep. *We* deserved better.

I glanced down at the video I held in my hands. And that's when it hit me. "I'll be right back," I said to Rosie.

I dashed upstairs and called Phoebe, even though it was pretty late. She answered on the second ring. "George Clooney," I said to her.

"What about him?"

"He's the perfect man for my mom."

— 7 —

The next morning the phone rang at nine, just like it did every Sunday. I was coming down the stairs, showered and dressed in my favorite jeans and a blue T-shirt that said NO LOGO on the front, and yes, I saw the irony. I'd tried spiking my hair up with some gel for an edgier look, but it was already starting to droop because Mom still hadn't had a chance to trim it and it was getting too long. She and Rosie were in the kitchen, putting frozen waffles into the toaster oven.

"Hi, Daddy," I heard Rosie say from the kitchen.

I'd managed to avoid talking to him since the Turd Incident, and I had no intention of caving in. Plus, I was dying to get Phoebe's perspective on my idea, which, in the cold light of day, seemed kind of far-fetched and possibly even delusional. So as Rosie settled into a long monologue, telling him about her week in minute detail, I wandered through the kitchen, said hi to Mom, poured myself a glass of juice, drank it, and strolled to the front door. I was slipping on my rubber boots and my rain jacket when Rosie approached, carrying the phone.

"It's Daddy." She held the phone out to me.

"Tell him I'm not here."

Rosie hesitated, still holding out the phone. "But you are here."

"No, I'm not."

"Yes, you are – you're right in front of me. He knows you're here. I told him you were here." She added in a dramatic whisper, "He can probably hear you telling me you're not here."

I just shrugged and raised my voice. "I'm not here."

Rosie's brow furrowed. She lifted the phone to her ear. "She says she's not here."

I rolled my eyes.

"I love you too, Daddy. Bye." Rosie hung up. "He sounded mad that you wouldn't talk to him."

"Whatever."

Rosie sighed heavily. "You shouldn't have fed poo to our sisters, Violet."

"They're not our sisters," I said. "They're our half sisters. And Dad's chosen to be with them instead of us because he loves them more. So do you think he really cares if we visit him or not?"

Rosie's face crumpled. Then the waterworks started – great big tears rolled down her cheeks. "He doesn't love them more! You shut up!" She picked one of my Converse shoes off the floor and threw it at my head, missing me by inches. Then she ran upstairs. A moment later, our bedroom door slammed.

"Violet, what's going on?" Mom called from the kitchen. "You'd better be talking to your father!"

"I'm going to Phoebe's, bye!" I shouted, as I dashed out the front door.

I knew I'd be in for it later. I knew Mom would probably ground me again for not apologizing to Dad and Jennica and the twins, and I knew she'd force me to apologize to Rosie and tell her I didn't mean it.

But I also knew that what I'd said to Rosie was the truth.

And sometimes, the truth hurts.

Cathy answered the door at Phoebe's house. She was dressed head to toe in spandex, just back from a run.

"Violet, hi. Günter's made pancakes. Come join us."

I slipped off my shoes and followed her inside. Frozen waffles were okay, but Günter's pancakes – home-made, thick, and fluffy – were superior in every way.

Their house was the exact opposite of ours, well-maintained and immaculate. Decorated in beiges and browns, all the furniture matched and none was second-hand. The rooms – even the kitchen, where Günter had just made pancakes – were sparkly clean and clutter-free.

After breakfast, Phoebe and I headed to her bedroom. Unlike the other rooms of the house, it looked like a bomb had exploded. All the clothes she'd worn for the past week littered the floor. Books were stacked in piles around the room. Three of her drawers were open, their contents spilling out. Her parents had given up trying to get her to keep her room tidy a long time ago, and now they just asked her to keep the door shut so they didn't have to look at it.

Two of her walls were covered with giant collages of skinny models from magazines. "Something to aspire to," she would say, which was crazy. Phoebe is gorgeous. She has long, straight, shiny black hair, perfect skin, and dark brown almond-shaped eyes. I would kill to have her looks. But Phoebe just couldn't see it, and it was all thanks to Thing One and Thing Two.

What happened was this: Phoebe and I had been hanging around the swings at recess in sixth grade when we'd heard giggling nearby. Ashley and Lauren were sitting at a picnic table, checking us out. Claudia was with them. Ashley leaned into Lauren and Claudia and whispered something, and Lauren burst into a fit of giggles. Claudia just rolled her eyes.

After school, we caught up to Claudia at her locker and asked her what Ashley had said about us.

"She gave you nicknames," Claudia told us as she blew an enormous bubble with her gum.

"What nicknames?" Phoebe asked.

"You really want to know?"

We nodded, but our stomachs clenched.

"Piggy and Pancake. *Pancake,* as in *'flat as a.'* And *Piggy,* as in . . . well. You know."

Claudia hadn't told us to be mean; she'd told us because we'd asked. But we felt like we'd been punched in the gut.

Phoebe even cried a little on the way home that day. "It's baby fat," she said. "Cathy says it'll disappear when I have a growth spurt."

"Your mom's right. And anyway, you're not fat. You're super-pretty."

"Yeah, right."

"It's true. And at least you didn't get called Pancake," I said, gazing down at my flat chest.

"Piggy is worse," she sniffed.

That night we'd nicknamed Ashley and Lauren Thing One and Thing Two. It didn't change anything, but it did make us both feel a little bit better.

———

Now that we were alone in her room, Phoebe agreed that my idea was a long shot. "George probably gets all sorts of proposals every day. Some might even include photos. You know – ones that leave nothing to the imagination."

She grabbed her laptop from under a pile of clothes on her bed and turned it on. "But, on the other hand, as Cathy likes to say, *nothing ventured, nothing gained*. And you have an ace up your sleeve: Your mom's already met him."

Phoebe punched *George Clooney* into the Google search engine. We got four million, four hundred thousand hits. This is what we learned.

GEORGE CLOONEY FACTS

1) *Not only is George C. a great actor, he is also an environmentalist and an advocate for lots of good causes.*
2) *He loves animals and had a Vietnamese potbellied pig for years. He was heartbroken when the pig died.*
3) *He's been voted sexiest man alive by People magazine, twice.*
4) *He is friends with that other over-forty hottie, Brad Pitt.*
5) *He is a practical joker.*
6) *He likes to ride motorcycles.*

7) He has a second home on Lake Como, in Italy.
8) He's been married once, a long time ago.
9) He's dated lots of women since then, mostly models.
10) He's vowed he will never marry again.

Number 10 was discouraging. "As Cathy also likes to say," Phoebe said philosophically, "*never say never.*"

"Maybe he just hasn't met the right woman."

Phoebe nodded. "Günter's told me lots of times, he never planned on getting roped into the institution of matrimony until Cathy swept him off his feet."

She opened up a blank Word document. "Worst-case scenario, you never hear from him. Best-case scenario, you do. Bottom line, you've got nothing to lose." She passed me her laptop. "I'll go play on the Wii with Günter. Call me when you're done."

This is what I wrote.

Dear Mr. Clooney,

Hello. How are you? I am fine. You don't know me, so please allow me to introduce myself.

My name is Violet Gustafson (first name because my mom loves flowers, last name because my mom has Swedish parents and after my folks divorced, she had her last name legally changed back to her maiden name and so did I). I am twelve years old. I live in Vancouver, Canada.

But enough about me. I'm really writing to tell you about my mom. Her name is Ingrid Gustafson, and if that name is ringing a bell, it's because you've met her. A long time ago, she did your hair on a movie set. You gave her an autographed picture that said To Ingrid – May Our Paths Cross Again. *Well, George (is it okay if I call you George?), this is your lucky day!*

My mom is awesome. She is thirty-seven years old and very pretty. Everyone says so. She has long brown hair and green eyes and only one slightly crooked tooth. She is average height, five feet five inches, and she has a pretty good body for someone who's given birth to two children. I won't lie to you, George, she could probably stand to lose a bit of the spare tire around her middle, but I ask you, how is she supposed to find the time to go to the gym when she is a working single parent raising two kids?

Like you, Ingrid has been married once before, to my dad, whose name is Ian Popischil. If his name is also ringing a bell, it's because he lives in Los Angeles too, so perhaps you've met. He's a TV director. Ian is remarried to an actress named Jennica Valentine. I suppose you may have met her too, but trust me, you never want to cast her in any of your movies because, to be blunt, she is not very talented. She was in a show once called Paranormal Pam *that got canceled after just three episodes, and since then she has just had little parts, like The Party Girl Who Gets Stabbed to Death in the First Two Minutes of* CSI Miami, *and one of Charlie's bimbos on* Two and a Half Men. *My dad and Jennica have twins, so the truth is, he doesn't have much time for us, but that's okay because I don't have much time for him either.*

Which brings me to the reason I'm writing. My parents split just over two years ago. At first, my mom didn't date at all. She just cried a lot and drank too much wine. But after a while, thanks to the lousy influence of her so-called friend Karen, she started dating again.

A lot.

The problem, George, is that her taste in men sucks. So I'm taking it upon myself to try to find someone more suitable for her. And I have a very good feeling about you. I am positive that you and my mom would really hit it off. You already did once, ha-ha.

I know you have had many girlfriends (my friend Phoebe says you are a "serial monogamist") and even one wife a long time ago and that nothing's really worked out for you. Well, have you ever stopped to consider that maybe you just haven't met the right woman? I hope you won't be insulted when I say that perhaps some of those glamorous model types you've dated were just using you for your fame and fortune. I wouldn't put it past them. They can be very calculating.

Just watch America's Next Top Model *and you will see what I'm talking about.*

My mom, on the other hand, would never use you. She is a talented hairstylist who would not expect you to be her sugar daddy (although I'm sure she wouldn't say no to the occasional trip to your place in Italy). My mom has always believed in making her own way in life, and no matter where you chose to live, she would get a job (but if I could also recommend, maybe she could work part-time, which would give her a chance to get to the gym and firm up that waistline and allow her to be at home when my sister and I get back from school).

Which brings me to my final point. I understand that you think you'll never have kids. Well, George, I can offer you the best of both worlds. You would have none of the muss and fuss of babies because you would be adopting two older daughters. As I mentioned, I am twelve and my sister, Rosie, is five. I believe we would make excellent stepchildren, and we would call you whatever you like, whether it's George or even Dad.

I am enclosing a photo of my mom so you can see that I'm not lying about her looks. I would appreciate a speedy response.

Sincerely,

Violet Gustafson

I called Phoebe into the room when the letter was done. She read it through, and together we made a few adjustments. "This is really good, Violet," she said, and I could tell she meant it. "He'd be nuts not to want to meet her after he reads this."

We printed the letter in Cathy's home office. Then we realized we needed George's address, so we Googled him again. His home address didn't seem to be listed, so we had to settle for his management company instead. I addressed the envelope to Mr. Clooney, care of his manager. We put about six stamps on the envelope, just to be safe.

Last but not least, I pulled out a photo from my jacket pocket. I'd taken it from the front of the *Wedding* video at home. Sure, it was a little dated, but I wanted a picture that would make a good first impression. Phoebe handed me a pair of scissors. I sliced Dad out of the photo, crumpled him up, and threw him in the garbage. Then I slipped Mom carefully into the envelope.

Phoebe and I put on our jackets and walked to the mailbox on the corner. For once, it wasn't raining. And as I dropped the envelope into the box, the sun broke through the clouds.

— 8 —

We had gym with Ms. Baldelli for first period on Monday mornings, so I took Rosie to her kindergarten class while Phoebe headed to the change room. Rosie was wearing her fairy wings again. I'd managed to fix the tear with a piece of duct tape. At first, Rosie hadn't been convinced.

"It doesn't look very nice," she'd said.

"What if I put a matching piece of tape on the other wing?" I'd suggested. "That way it will look like a matching silver marking." That had done the trick.

As I put her backpack into her cubby, she whispered to me, "That's Isabelle, the girl who tore my wings." I glanced over. Isabelle was a few cubbies down. A couple of girls were gathered around her, and she was showing them her shoes. They were pink, and when she walked, little lights lit up around the heels.

Then she spotted Rosie. "What's that on your wings?" she asked.

"Silver marking," Rosie replied.

"No, it's not. It's tape!" Isabelle retorted. "It looks dumb." Then she turned her back on Rosie and bounced up and down on her shoes.

Rosie took her wings off and handed them to me. "I've changed my mind. I don't want to wear them today." She stuck her thumb in her mouth and headed into class.

I wanted to throttle Isabelle. Or at least pinch her, hard. Instead, I smiled as I walked past her and her little posse.

"Great shoes," I said. "If you're three."

Yeah. I know. Putting down a five-year-old is cheap, but it still felt good. I left the room with a spring in my step, slinging Rosie's wings over my shoulder, and smacked right into Jean-Paul.

"Hey, *Pamplemousse*. You plan on flying away?" he asked, glancing at the wings.

Pamplemousse? "They're my sister's."

"They go with your shoes," he continued, indicating my pink and white polka-dot high tops. "You love Converse, huh?"

I nodded. "I have six pairs." We started walking down the stairs together toward the change rooms, and I tried to remind myself that this was an entirely normal and non-meaningful thing to do and that my body could stop feeling all tingly.

"Where do you get them?"

"My dad sends them to me from L.A. They're cheaper there."

"Your folks are divorced?"

I nodded.

"Mine, too. My dad's still in Winnipeg." We arrived outside the change rooms. "Well. See you in gym," he said, then he made a face. "I hear we're doing line dancing."

I pushed open the door to the girls' change room. Phoebe was already in her gym shorts. I must've looked like I was in shock or something because she said to me, "What? What's wrong?"

"Nothing's wrong," I said. Then, as nonchalantly as I could: "Jean-Paul just talked to me. He called me *Pamplemousse*."

"He called you Grapefruit! That is adorable!"

"Please," I said. "He was just being nice."

Phoebe simply smiled, an annoying smug little grin.

"Hey, Violet." Ashley and Lauren appeared from around the corner, where the mirrors were. I could tell from their faces that they'd been slathering on makeup. For gym.

"Guess who I saw this morning?" Ashley continued, smirking.

"How would I know?"

"Your mom. Outside Bean Around the World."

"So?"

"So, she was making out with some dorky-looking guy with red hair."

Oh. I pulled my gym shirt over my head, hoping to hide what I knew was a bright red face.

"Your mom gets around, doesn't she?" Ashley said. "Remember last year, when she dated our sub?"

Groan. As if I could forget.

What happened was this: In sixth grade, we'd had a sub for a few weeks. His name was Paulo Cassini, and he filled in for our teacher while she dealt with a family emergency. Mom met him at parent-teacher night, and he started making eyes at her. Right in front of me. Right in front of a few of the other parents. It was barf-inducing.

They only went out a handful of times because he was a Dungeons and Dragons fanatic, and it was all he ever talked about. Their short dating history might have remained yet another yucky-but-brief Gustafson Family Secret if Ashley and some of her friends hadn't seen them together at the Park Theater one night, standing in the popcorn line, holding hands.

Honestly, parent-teacher dating should be outlawed.

"If I were you," Ashley said now as she applied one more layer of lip gloss, "I'd want my mom to nip the PDA's in the butt."

"Bud," I muttered.

"What?"

"Nip the PDA's in the *bud*. You said *butt*."

Ashley gave a dismissive laugh. "Come on, Lauren," she said, and Thing Two obediently followed Thing One out of the room.

Claudia was sitting next to Phoebe, wrapping her big wad of gum in a piece of paper so she could reuse it later. "You're lucky," she said to me. "I wish my mom was still playing the field. She hooked up with my stepdad two months after my dad left. He's a total jerk-face. Soon as I'm sixteen, I am out of there."

The door to the gym swung open, and Ms. Baldelli blew her whistle. "Girls, get a move on!"

We were spared doing line dancing because Ms. Baldelli forgot her CD player. She made us play dodge-ball instead. Every ball I threw was aimed at Ashley's head, but no matter how hard I tried, I never hit her.

But she got me in the nether regions. Twice.

"So, Violet. What do you think of this new guy your mom's seeing?" Karen asked me, without glancing up from her laptop. She was sitting in one of the salon chairs, her feet crossed under her. Phoebe and I sat beside her at my mom's workstation, flipping through copies of *US* magazine and *Entertainment Weekly.* Rosie sat in her favorite chair farther down, spinning in circles. Once in a while, I would glance up at George Clooney's grinning face and try to send him positive vibes.

I looked straight at Karen and pretended to stick a finger down my throat.

"You don't like any of your mom's boyfriends," Karen replied.

"That's because they're all losers."

"Hey. I set her up with some of those so-called losers."

"Yeah, and they were the worst ones of all."

Karen gave me the hairy eyeball, but she didn't contradict me because she knew I spoke the truth. She'd set my mom up with Carl, the first guy Mom had dated post-Dad. He seemed like a sweet funny guy at first. But Mom quickly found out that he went all Jekyll and Hyde when he drank. After she told him she didn't want to see him anymore, he showed up at our house one night, drunk as a skunk. Mom wasn't home. When I refused to let him in (*duh*), he picked up a rock and hurled it through our front window.

The Brights saw it happen. They were the ones who called the cops. We never saw Carl again.

Karen was also the one who set my mom up with Jonathan. In some ways, Jonathan had been the worst of all.

"She seems to like him," Karen said now. "What's his last name again? Frankfurter?"

"Wiener," I said. "Dudley Wiener."

Karen cackled. "That's a truly unfortunate name."

"Shouldn't you be working or something?" I said. My mom was helping Mohamed give a woman a perm a few chairs down.

"I'm here if the students need me," she replied. "I'm just checking my Facebook page. Speaking of which, how come you haven't friended me yet?"

Phoebe and I peered at each other over our magazines. We were both on Facebook; all the kids at school were. Personally, the thrill of Facebook had worn off pretty quickly for me, possibly because I had just nine friends and one was Phoebe and one was my mom. I only checked my page about once a week. So when I'd logged on last week and seen *1 friend request*, I won't lie, I was kind of excited. Until I found out the request was from Karen. The urge to hit IGNORE was overwhelming. But instead I hadn't hit CONFIRM or IGNORE. I just logged out instead.

"Oh," I lied, "did you try to friend me? I haven't been on in such a long time."

"Well, friend me back. I'm about to break the three hundred mark."

Honestly, it was hard to believe Karen was in her late thirties sometimes.

Mohamed had just put his client under a hair-dryer, so Mom came and joined us. She was wearing a shirt that covered her spare tire today, which was a relief.

"Do you want that trim now?" she asked me.

"Sure, thanks."

Karen made a face as my mom started trimming my hair. "It looks better longer, Violet. You should let it grow out. Boys like girls with long hair."

"Then this is perfect because I don't want boys to like me."

"Why? Are you gay?"

"Karen –" my mom began.

"I'm not gay," I replied. "I'm just not interested."

"Seriously? Man, I was boy crazy by the time I was five," Karen said, chuckling at the memory.

"Yeah, and look where that's got you."

Phoebe snorted from behind her magazine. Karen opened her mouth to retort, but Mom cut her off. "Enough, you two. Violet, remember you have to call your dad when you get home."

I didn't answer.

"I'm serious. After making your sister lie for you yesterday . . ."

"She didn't lie. She said, *She says she's not here.*"

"Don't argue with me. He's expecting your call after school today." She tugged gently on my ear. "You can't avoid him forever, Violet. You need to clear the air."

"Don't tell me you still haven't apologized?" asked Karen, incredulous.

"Shut up, Karen," I replied. Which was just another way of saying no.

When we got home, I gave Rosie a glass of milk and a granola bar from the Costco mega-pack in the cupboard and sent her down to the basement to watch a video. Then I ran upstairs to my bedroom and grabbed my Magic 8 Ball.

Phoebe was already sitting on the gold couch when I came into the living room. I sat on the red couch.

"Are you sure about this?" Phoebe asked.

I shrugged. "It'll keep things interesting. Ready?"

"Ready."

I picked up the phone and dialed.

"Hello?" I heard my dad's voice on the other end. So did Phoebe, since I had us on speakerphone.

I didn't reply.

"Violet, is that you? We have call display."

I shook the Magic 8 Ball. *"It is decidedly so."*

"I'm glad you called. We have lots to talk about. How are you?"

I shook it again. *"Ask again later."*

There was a pause. "Hey, I'm directing an episode of *Glamour Girl* starting next week. Isn't it your favorite show?"

It was. But since the Magic 8 Ball was providing my answers, I said, *"Don't count on it."*

There was another pause. I could tell he was trying really hard not to sound frustrated, which gave me a great deal of satisfaction. "Yeah, I guess your favorite shows change all the time. Too bad, I got you Carly Joseph's autograph."

Phoebe and I looked at each other, our eyes wide. We loved Carly Joseph.

"Maybe I'll send it anyway. If you don't want it, Rosie might."

"It is certain."

There was another pause. "Are you answering me from a Magic 8 Ball?"

"Signs point to yes."

"Well, cut it out, okay?" he said, and this time he didn't hide his frustration. "We have to talk about what happened when you were here. Jennica's still really upset, and no wonder. You owe all of us an apology, Violet. Especially your little sisters."

I shook the Magic 8 Ball. *"My reply is no."*

Dad took a deep breath. "Look. You and your sister are supposed to be coming down for March Break. But until you apologize . . . I can't allow it."

To be honest, this stung a little, but I kept my expression neutral for Phoebe's sake.

"How could you have done it, Violet?" he continued. "They're *two years old.* They're your sisters, for crying out loud!" He sounded genuinely upset now.

Phoebe covered her face with her hands, peering through the cracks between her fingers like she was watching a horror movie.

I didn't answer. Part of me wanted to shout that of course I was sorry, that I knew it was a terrible thing I'd done. But part of me wanted to shout that what he'd done to us was *so much worse,* and nobody had ever made him apologize.

"Fine," he said. "I'm done. Just remember that I love you."

I shook the ball one last time. *"Highly doubtful,"* I said. Then I hung up.

Phoebe looked at me, a cushion crushed against her chest. "Wow," she said. "That was better than TV." She shook her head. "You're truly awful."

But the way she said it, I could tell it was a compliment.

— 9 —

After Dad moved to Los Angeles to be with Jennica, I made like a turtle and went into my shell. I spent most of my spare time alone in my room, reading or doing weird obsessive reorganizing of our clothes, our books, our toys. When I was done with the stuff in our room, I'd sneak into Mom's room and organize her shoes by color, or line up everything in the medicine cabinet in the bathroom according to size. It wasn't so much about cleaning as it was about wanting everything to be in its proper place.

Phoebe tried to pull me out of myself for the first couple of weeks, but when she realized it wasn't working, did she abandon me? No. She'd just come over with a book of her own, and the two of us would read in my room for hours without talking. If I needed to take some time out to reorganize all the towels and sheets in our linen closet, she wouldn't say a word. We traded books we liked, and by the end of those first few months, I'd read the *Narnia* series, the *Alice, I Think* trilogy, plus everything Judy Blume and Roald Dahl had ever written.

Mom was worried about me, but she had a lot of other stuff on her plate. She had to look after Rosie; she had to think about going back to work; and she was dealing with her own grief. At first I thought *grief* was a weird word to use because it wasn't like my dad had died or anything. But Amanda explained to me one night that *grief* was the perfect word.

"Your mom has suffered a big loss. You all have."

I didn't tell Amanda that I sometimes wished Dad *was* dead. Killed in a car crash, or struck by lightning. I thought it would be easier to grieve if he was dead and buried, instead of alive and well and living in L.A. with a bimbo who was about to give him a new set of children to love.

Eventually, on Amanda's advice, my mom sent me to a therapist to help me work through my feelings. The therapist's name was Dr. Belinda Boniface, which was a pretty fabulous name. She was nice enough, I guess. I only went a handful of times because Dr. Belinda Boniface charged a lot of money for her services, which didn't make a lot of sense to me since all she did was ask questions and watch me play with dolls.

One day she asked me to draw a picture of our family. This is what I drew.

She noticed that my dad wasn't in the picture, so she asked me to draw a picture of him. This is what I drew.

Afterward, Dr. Belinda Boniface told my mom that these drawings indicated that I was feeling a lot of anger toward my dad.

Duh, I remembered thinking. I hardly needed expensive therapy for someone to tell me that.

— 10 —

“hat’s your alias?” I asked Phoebe.

“Nancy,” she said.

“As in Drew?”

“But, of course.”

“And what are you looking for?”

“A gift for my mom’s birthday.”

It was a Tuesday night, and Rosie and I were hanging out at Phoebe’s house. We’d just demolished one of Cathy’s delicious stir-fries and were working our way through wedges of Günter’s apple pie. We’d come by after school so I could do a couple of loads of laundry, and when Cathy had heard that my mom was going out with Dudley again, she’d invited us to stay for dinner.

“Remember to bring binoculars,” Phoebe said.

“Binoculars, check.”

"I'll bring walkie-talkies."

"Walkie-talkies, check. I'll bring sandwiches."

"And I'll bring cookies and juice boxes."

"I like Dudley," Rosie piped up, her mouth full of pie.

"I know you do. But we have to make sure he doesn't have any nasty secrets. Remember Jonathan?"

"He hurted Mom's feelings."

"Exactly. We don't want that to happen again, do we?"

Rosie shook her head. She stuffed her last bite of pie into her mouth, then jumped out of her chair to find Günter, who'd promised to play a game with her on the Wii.

"You know, we wouldn't need to do any of this if George would just answer my letter," I said. It had been almost a month since I'd sent it, and I still didn't have a response.

Phoebe shrugged. "He's probably really busy. Anyway, I'm glad we're doing this. I'll finally get to see what The Wiener looks like."

I sighed. "He looks like a wiener."

I couldn't believe my mom was still seeing Dudley. She definitely wasn't doing it for his looks. And she certainly wasn't doing it for his stupid gifts. We were now the proud owners of a matching toothbrush holder to go with the soap dish, bathtub stickers, a toilet brush

(! seriously), and toilet paper with hearts printed all over it.

And she couldn't be seeing him for his money because if he had any, he clearly didn't like to spend it.

"We went to a free jazz concert in a church," Mom told us one night.

Or, "We went for a long walk down at Jericho Beach in the rain."

Or, "He took me to a free lecture by the Tree-Hugging Granny."

And she absolutely, positively wasn't seeing him for his sense of humor. I'd recently had my darkest suspicions confirmed: Dudley was a punster.

While he'd waited for Mom to get ready one night, Dudley played Go Fish with Rosie in the living room. "This game is starting to give me a *haddock,*" he said. "Hey, you just had your *tuna.* Do you think I *cod* have my *tuna* now?" Rosie, of course, thought this kind of wordplay was hilarious. He had her in hysterics. When Mom joined them, he said, "Rosie's giving me a *halibut* hard time here, Ingrid."

Mom had actually giggled.

"You do realize that puns are the lowest form of humor," I said.

He'd nodded happily. "I know. But sometimes I just can't help myself. I love words! I love the English language."

Then stop massacring it! I'd wanted to shout.

Tonight The Wiener had taken my mom to the Vancouver Art Gallery. Why? Because it was pay-what-you-can Tuesday. Phoebe and I had decided that since the next day was a Professional Development day and we didn't have to go to school, we would seize the opportunity to spy on Dudley.

It wouldn't be the first time we'd spied on one of Mom's boyfriends, and we were quite good at it. We'd read the ultimate detective handbook, *Harriet the Spy*, at least three times each. And between us, we'd devoured a bunch of Sherlock Holmes stories and about ten of the Nancy Drew mysteries, after I'd discovered a box full of them at a yard sale two summers ago. Nancy was a little outdated, but some of her techniques were still relevant.

Most of Mom's dates had simply provided a chance for Phoebe and me to perfect my list of questions for interrogation purposes. For example, we didn't add the question about addictions until after Carl, and we only added *Are you married?* after Larry the Unibrow. Most of them hadn't lasted long enough for us to go into detective mode. Except for two.

CASE #1: GUY FORNIER

Guy was pronounced the French way, like "Gee" with a hard G. Mom met him on Havalife. Guy had lots of thick black hair and designer glasses, which made him look smarter than he really was. He wore expensive suits and worked in an office building downtown, and he must have made a lot of money because he drove a very expensive sports car that had only two seats, which was the first clue that he wasn't child-friendly.

Guy hated Rosie and me. Oh, he'd fake it in front of my mom, but whenever she left the room, he'd go all cold and weird. Once, I'd simply asked him if he had a criminal record or any aliases we should know about, and he'd said to me, "Too bad your mom couldn't put you up for adoption."

The thought of him becoming a more permanent part of our lives made me feel sick. So Phoebe and I took a page out of Sherlock Holmes and *The Hound of the Baskervilles*: We set a trap.

Next time Guy was scheduled to pick Mom up, Phoebe and I bought a chocolate cake mix and told Rosie we were going to bake him a cake. We let Rosie add the water and the egg and stir. By the time she was done, her hands and face were covered in batter.

The doorbell rang because it was still working back then. "I'll get it!" Rosie shouted, running out of the room.

Phoebe and I followed. We watched from the hallway as Rosie did what we knew she would. She launched herself at Guy and threw her arms around him.

He looked down at his white-and-blue pin-striped

shirt and navy jacket, which were both covered in brown handprints. His face twisted with anger.

FOR THE RECORD: If I'd had any idea what he was going to do next, I would never, ever have sent my sister into the line of fire.

He grabbed her and smacked her on the bum. Once. Twice.

Phoebe and I were so shocked, we couldn't speak. I wanted to tear out his thick black hair. Rosie, of course, burst into tears.

Mom tore down the stairs. "What happened?" She grabbed Rosie, who was sobbing by now, and hugged her tight, not caring for one moment that she, too, was getting covered in batter.

"He hit her," I whispered.

"What?"

"She got chocolate all over my suit!" Guy shouted. "This is Hugo Boss!"

Mom flipped. She told him that he was never, *ever* to lay a hand on her child. He told her he'd be sending her the dry-cleaning bill. She told him that he could take his dry-cleaning bill and shove it up his bum, except she didn't use the word *bum*.

Needless to say, we never saw Guy again. Case #1 closed.

Of all the guys my mom dated post-Dad, he was the one who came closest to sweeping her off her feet. And she wasn't the only one who fell for him – we all did. He was handsome; he was a successful lawyer; and he liked Rosie and me. He'd always show up with flowers for my mom and little toys for us.

Karen introduced Mom to Jonathan at a party, and they hit it off right away. I could tell that Mom was really falling for him because our house hadn't been that clean since before Dad left. Jonathan was a neat and tidy kind of guy, so even though she'd be pooped after work, Mom would get out the vacuum cleaner or the duster and clean for a while. I even saw her wash the floors once or twice.

Jonathan would take her out at least twice a week, and he would have supper with us at least once a week, and he would call her every night before she went to sleep.

I even started telling my dad about Jonathan on our Sunday-morning phone calls. "He's a great guy. Super-handsome. He makes tons of money. And he treats Mom really, really well."

"*Huh*. Well, that's great," he'd say, and I could tell that only part of him meant it.

"We spend a lot of time with him, actually. Way more time than we do with you."

I laid it on pretty thick.

I even started fantasizing about what it would be like if Jonathan became our stepdad. I'd lie in bed at night thinking about it, and it would help me fall asleep. *We'll probably move to a much nicer house,* I'd think. *Maybe he'll teach me how to play basketball.* My dad had promised to do this with me, then he'd left. *Maybe he'll kiss us on our foreheads at bedtime, along with my mom, and leave the hall light on for Rosie until she falls asleep. Maybe he'll let me ride on his shoulders once in a while, even though I'm getting too big.*

But after they'd been dating for about four months, things cooled off. There were nights when he didn't phone. Sometimes my mom would call him, but there would be no answer. Then he started canceling some of their plans, saying he had to work late.

That's when Phoebe and I decided to walk in the footsteps of Harriet the Spy.

The next time Jonathan canceled a date with my mom, Phoebe told her parents she was going to my house to study. I told my mom I was going to Phoebe's house to study. Armed with binoculars and plenty of snacks, we took a bus to Jonathan's condo in the West End. It was a really nice place, right across the street from English Bay, with a tree growing on the roof. We stood on the beach side of the street, and from our position we could see right into his second-floor apartment. The blinds were open, but he wasn't home.

We hung out for over an hour. Because it was spring, it was still light out, even though by this time it was eight o'clock. The hot-dog vendor nearby kept giving us funny looks. We were just about to pack it in when we saw Jonathan. He was walking down the street arm in arm with a woman in a short black skirt and high heels. He took out his keys, and they disappeared into his building together.

"Maybe it's his sister," Phoebe said.

A few minutes later, we saw them in his apartment. We both lifted our binoculars to get a better look.

Jonathan and the woman started to make out, right in front of the window. After a few minutes, Jonathan closed the blinds.

"Probably not his sister," Phoebe said.

We lowered our binoculars. For some reason, I had an overwhelming urge to cry. That wasn't just my mom's boyfriend up there with another woman. It was my fantasy stepfather.

So I did cry. The hot-dog vendor stared at us. Phoebe bought two dogs from him, and he handed me a stack of extra napkins so I could blow my nose. The two of us headed back to the bus stop, eating our hot dogs and wondering how we were going to break the news to my mom.

What happened was this: The next time Jonathan came for dinner, I invited Phoebe over for moral support. When we were halfway through the meal, I just came right out and asked, "So, Jonathan, who was that woman you were with last week?"

Jonathan looked at me, perplexed. "What woman?"

"You know, the one you were kissing in your apartment."

Jonathan almost choked on his pasta. "You have quite the active imagination, Violet." He tried smiling, but he just looked constipated.

"Violet, what are you talking about?" my mom said in a quiet voice. Rosie had gone really quiet, too.

I didn't answer. I just looked at Jonathan, my heart racing. I was hoping there might actually be a logical explanation.

But all he said was "I don't want to discuss this in front of the kids."

So Mom made the three of us go upstairs.

We could hear the yelling from our bedroom. Poor Rosie was in tears. "Why would he kiss another lady when he could kiss Mommy any time he wants?" she asked.

Phoebe and I tried to take her mind off things by playing Operation with her, but Rosie just threw the wrenched ankle and the broken heart down an air vent. Then she had a tantrum and locked herself in the bathroom, and Phoebe and I couldn't get her out.

Jonathan left about fifteen minutes later, and Mom came upstairs with a screwdriver and took off the whole doorknob in order to get Rosie out. After she'd rocked Rosie to sleep, she told Phoebe and me to come downstairs. I don't know what I was expecting, but I figured at the very least we'd get a thank-you.

Nope. Mom was furious with us – for lying to her and to Phoebe's parents and for spying on Jonathan. But she never saw him again.

Mom wasn't herself for quite a while after that. She called in sick to work for a full week and barely left her bed. I took over making breakfast and packing lunches for Rosie and me and getting us out the door for school, and, come to think of it, I've been doing all of those things ever since. When we'd come home, Mom would still be in her robe, her hair unwashed. After the third day, she started to smell a little. Karen and Amanda took turns coming over in the evenings. Amanda would bring different herbal teas; Karen would bring booze.

It was like the whole thing with my dad all over again, but in some ways, this was even worse.

"It's the cumulative effect," Amanda tried to explain to me one night. "I think she's wondering if all the men she decides to trust will disappoint her in the end."

"Maybe I shouldn't have told her," I said.

Amanda sighed. "You were trying to do the right thing. Your mom knows that."

After a week, Mom went back to work, but I'd still catch her crying at the weirdest moments, like when we'd all be watching reruns of *Friends*. I wasn't doing too great, either. One day, I locked myself in the bathroom and cut off all my hair. I don't know why I did it, I just had this urge. A few days later, I vowed to myself that I would never, ever have a boyfriend.

"That's ridiculous," Phoebe said when I told her.

I shrugged. "A lot of single women lead rich and fulfilling lives."

"How are things going with your mom and Jonathan?" my dad asked the next time we spoke. My mom was in the room, reading a magazine.

"Actually," I said, "they broke up." My mom glanced up from her magazine.

There was silence on the other end for a moment. "What happened?"

"Jonathan was putting pressure on her," I told him, looking my mom in the eye. "He wanted to settle down and get married. Mom wasn't ready to get that serious. She *loves* being single."

"Oh," Dad replied. "Oh."

For the first time in weeks, my mom smiled.

— 11 —

"Subject is female, approximately forty years of age, mildly attractive if you ignore her pear shape. Over," Phoebe said through the walkie-talkie. She was walking outside Dudley's store, which was at Eleventh and Main. The store was called, I kid you not, Skip to My Loo.

Since I was the recognizable one, I was on the other side of the street, crouched behind a newspaper box. I peered at the store through my binoculars. I could just make out Dudley, talking to the pear-shaped woman.

"They don't seem to know each other," Phoebe said through the walkie. "I think she's looking for towels. Over."

Sure enough, five minutes later the woman left the store with a great big shopping bag.

I lowered the binoculars and sighed. We'd been on

our stakeout for over an hour, and, in spite of the clear skies and my extra fleece, I was bored and cold. Contrary to what TV shows make you believe, detective work can be a snore.

"Hi, *Pamplemousse*."

I almost jumped out of my skin. Jean-Paul stood over me. He was wearing his bomber jacket and jeans, with a gray-and-blue scarf around his neck and a matching toque on his head.

He looked spectacular. From a strictly objective perspective, of course.

"Jean-Paul!" I squeaked. "What are you doing here?"

"My guitar teacher lives a few blocks away. I booked an extra lesson since we had the day off school." I finally registered the guitar case he was carrying. And I called myself a detective.

"Who are you spying on?"

"What makes you think I'm spying on anyone?"

"You're crouched behind a newspaper box with binoculars around your neck and a walkie-talkie in your hand."

"I'm not –"

The walkie crackled to life. "Is that Jean-Paul?" said Phoebe's disembodied voice. "Did you tell him we're in the middle of a stakeout? Over."

I sighed. "No, but I will now. Over."

Phoebe crossed the street to join us, and the three of us ducked into a coffee shop. Jean-Paul ordered a hot chocolate, and Phoebe and I split a tea since we only had a toonie. At first, I just told him the basics: that Dudley was my mom's new boyfriend and we wanted to make sure he was legit. But Jean-Paul asked a lot of questions, and next thing I knew, I'd poured out the whole story – about my dad leaving us for Jennica; about Guy; about Jonathan.

When I was finished, he was really quiet.

"I guess it sounds crazy," I said, and I suddenly felt a huge knot in my stomach. *What if Jean-Paul wasn't as nice as he seemed? What if he chose to blab everything I'd just told him to the other kids at school?* Phoebe and I were already far enough down the food chain. We didn't need something like this to send us tumbling even farther.

"Before we left Winnipeg," he said, "my mom was dating this guy for a while. Jack. I couldn't stand him. He tried to boss me around all the time. I was almost relieved when she got the job out here – even though it took me away from my dad – because it took us far away from Jack."

He looked me right in the eye. "So, no, I don't think you're crazy. You're just trying to protect your family, right?"

"Right!"

Phoebe squeezed my thigh under the table, and I knew we were both thinking the same thing: Jean-Paul was one hundred percent awesomeness. From a strictly objective perspective, of course.

When we'd finished our drinks, Phoebe said, "I'm going to go into the store now."

"I can go in too," Jean-Paul said. "When Phoebe gets back."

Phoebe and I looked at him, surprised. "You don't have to do that," I said.

"I want to. It would be fun, going undercover."

So we agreed: Phoebe would go in first to see what she could find out, and Jean-Paul would go in after her. And while Phoebe was in the shop, Jean-Paul and I would crouch down behind the newspaper box across the street. Just the two of us. Alone, together.

I could hardly wait. From a strictly objective perspective, of course.

Phoebe, *aka* Nancy, had been gone for about ten minutes. Jean-Paul and I sat on the cold pavement across the street, our knees so close they were almost touching. I wracked my brain to think of something to say. "Do you like Vancouver?"

Yup. That was the best I could come up with.

"It's okay. Believe it or not, I miss Winnipeg winters. I know it's a lot warmer here, but the rain . . . I always feel damp and cold. And the days are so short and dark . . . I mean, the cold freezes your nose hairs in Winnipeg, but at least you see the sun once in a while."

"Do you miss your dad?"

"All the time. How about you?"

I shrugged. "He's been gone for over two years."

"That doesn't answer the question."

"I hate him."

"Still doesn't answer the question."

I looked down at my mittens. "Yes," I said. "I miss him."

"What do you miss about him?"

I thought about that for a moment. "He used to watch Saturday morning cartoons with me and Rosie. He'd bring us big bowls of cereal to eat in front of the TV, and he'd sing along with all the theme songs from *Arthur, The Magic School Bus, Caillou. . . .*"

"I loved *Caillou.*"

"And he taught me how to ride my bike. He'd take me for long bike rides sometimes, just the two of us. He gave great back rubs and was really good at fixing things. And he made up these stories, just for me, at bedtime. . . ."

My voice caught in my throat. I'd tried not to think about those stories for a long time. They were adventure tales, and Dad had made them up out of thin air. They'd always star me and my imaginary friend, Pete. The stories always started the same: Pete and I would go out to play in the backyard, and very quickly we'd get into some kind of mischief. Like we'd explore a hollow tree and fall down a hole that would take us to a magical kingdom. Or we'd jump in a puddle that suddenly turned into an ocean, and we'd find ourselves aboard a pirate ship. They were thrilling, always just a little bit scary, but of course everything always turned out okay, and each story would end with Pete and me walking through the back door just in time for milk and cookies.

By the time Dad left, he hardly ever told a Pete and Violet story – I was almost ten, after all. But every once in a while, when I'd had a particularly crappy day, he'd perch on the edge of my bed and just start talking. Sometimes I would groan and tell him I was too old for storytelling, but he'd just smile and continue, and I'd shut up and listen to his voice and feel safe.

I got over myself and turned to Jean-Paul. "What about you? What do you miss about your dad?"

"My dad's a great cook. I miss his *tourtière* and his roasts. I miss playing hockey with him on the ice rink near our house. I even miss hearing him sing Céline Dion songs at the top of his lungs in the shower."

"Ugh," I said, laughing. "Why did they get divorced?"

"They fought all the time. I don't think they liked each other very much."

"My parents never fought. They were like best friends. They were always hugging and kissing in front of us . . . then, *boom,* Dad tells us he's in love with another woman. It makes you start thinking. Was *everything* a lie? Like, did he actually hate *Caillou*?"

"Nobody could hate *Caillou*."

And suddenly Jean-Paul grabbed my hand and squeezed it, just for a fraction of a second, before he let go. It happened so fast, I wasn't completely sure it *had* happened.

"Hey. I'm back." It was Phoebe. She crouched down beside us.

"Anything interesting?"

"Zip. Sorry, Violet."

I turned to Jean-Paul. "You don't have to go in."

Jean-Paul shrugged. "I want to." He jumped up and made his way to the corner. When the light changed, he walked across the street and disappeared into Skip to My Loo.

"So? How did things go?" Phoebe asked as she pulled a cheese sandwich out of my backpack.

"Fine," I said, trying to sound cool.

"Fine?"

"Fine."

"Then why are you as red as a beet?"

I sighed. I couldn't hide anything from Phoebe. "I think he momentarily held my hand," I told her.

"Oh. My. *God!!*" Then she shrieked so loud, I had to cover my ears. "I knew it! I knew he liked you, and I *know* you like him."

I couldn't deny it. Phoebe was right. I *did* like him. From a strictly objective perspective, of course.

When Jean-Paul came back, he was carrying a bar of lavender soap in a small bag.

"Did you learn anything?"

"Aside from the fact that Dudley thinks this soap will have my mom in a *lather*? Nothing. Sorry."

Our mission completed, the three of us walked slowly up Main Street together. We reached Jean-Paul's street first.

"That was fun," he said. "If you do any more stake-outs, let me know."

He'd just started walking away when I saw them, standing on the other side of the street.

Ashley and Lauren. Thing One and Thing Two. They were staring at us in disbelief.

It was a perfect ending to a perfect day.

— 12 —

That night, after I'd made fish sticks and frozen peas and toast for Rosie and me because Mom was out with Dudley, and after I'd forced Rosie to eat all her peas because she needed her vegetables, and after I'd washed the dishes and read to Rosie until she'd fallen into a deep sleep, I decided to check my Facebook account before *Glamour Girl* started at nine.

I logged in with my password, *badattitude1*.

I could hardly believe it. I had *3 friend requests*.

The first was Karen's old request. I sighed heavily. Then I pressed CONFIRM.

The second request was from Claudia. I pressed CONFIRM.

The third request was from Ashley Anderson.

Yes, *that* Ashley Anderson.

I stared at her profile photo, feeling confused, suspicious, and oddly flattered all at once. *Why would Thing One want to friend me?*

I moved the arrow to IGNORE.

Then I thought, *Maybe, when she saw Phoebe and me with Jean-Paul, she realized we aren't total bottom-feeders after all. Maybe this is her way of saying so.*

I moved the arrow to CONFIRM.

Then I thought, *This is the girl who nicknamed you Pancake! The girl who loves to embarrass you in front of the entire class!*

I moved the arrow to IGNORE again.

Then I thought, *But I've already confirmed Claudia as a friend. If I ignore Ashley, she'll find out and might make my life even more miserable.*

I let out a groan. *Who knew Facebook could be so complicated?*

Suddenly Rosie cried from upstairs, "Violet? I forgot to put on my pull-ups and I peed!"

"Coming!"

I stood up, looking one last time at Ashley's friend request.

Just before I dashed upstairs to change Rosie's sheets, I pressed CONFIRM.

— 13 —

"Did Ashley friend you last night on Facebook?" I asked Phoebe, after we'd dropped off Rosie at kindergarten.

"No. As if."

"She friended me."

Phoebe raised her eyebrows. "Tell me you hit IGNORE."

"Of course."

Phoebe's eyes narrowed. "You know I can check when I get home. As your Facebook friend, I have access to your friend list."

I sighed. "Fine. I hit CONFIRM."

Phoebe stopped walking. "You friended her? After the way she's treated us?"

I shrugged. "I sort of took it as a good sign, you know?"

"Violet. This is the girl who nicknamed you *Pancake*. Who called me *Piggy* –"

"Hey, guys, check it out."

Claudia was beckoning to us from the landing halfway up the stairs, where she was putting up posters. Relieved to have a subject change, I hurried to join her.

SADIE HAWKINS DANCE, the poster read in capital letters. WEDNESDAY, MARCH 13, 7:00 P.M.

"What's a Sadie Hawkins Dance?" I asked.

"It's where the girls have to ask the boys," she told us, rolling her eyes. "It wasn't my idea. Paula Michalowski came up with it." Claudia was on the Social Committee, so she was very in-the-know.

"Who was Sadie Hawkins?" asked Phoebe.

Claudia shrugged. "Some girl who couldn't get a date the normal way, I guess. Anyway, you guys should come. I'm going to invite Jonah."

"I suppose I could invite Andrew," Phoebe said as we climbed the stairs. Andrew was the guy who'd done the presentation on Scottish clans. Phoebe had known him since they were both in diapers because they'd gone to the same daycare. "And you," she continued, "could invite Jean-Paul."

"No," I replied firmly, "I couldn't."

Before Phoebe could argue with me about what she liked to call "your cynical and completely unrealistic pact with yourself," Ashley and Lauren materialized in front of us like specters, blocking our path.

"Oh, hey, Violet," said Ashley. "Phyllis."

"Phoebe," Phoebe answered hotly. "We've only been going to the same school since kindergarten."

Ashley ignored her and turned her attention to me. "You have a good day off yesterday?"

"Great."

"Saw you with Jean-Paul," she said. "You guys just happen to run into each other, or what?"

"Nope," Phoebe said smugly. "We hung out with him. For hours. Right, Violet?"

"Right."

Ashley gave us a thin smile. "He's *sooo* nice, don't you think?"

Phoebe and I glanced at each other, our senses on high alert. We could both smell a trap.

"Yeah," I replied warily.

"That's one of his best qualities. He's nice to *everyone*, even if he has no interest in them whatsoever."

"Oh," replied Phoebe. "You mean he's been nice to you, too?"

I tried to swallow a laugh, and it came out as a snort instead.

"Anyways –" Ashley started.

"*Anyway*," I said.

"Pardon?"

"It's *anyway. Anyways* isn't really a word." Yup. It was like my own personalized form of Tourette's Syndrome.

"You are *such* a loser, Pancake," she said, using my nickname to my face for the first time ever. "And your hair sucks."

Thing One and Thing Two swept past us to their lockers. I touched my hair self-consciously; I'd tried the gel thing again and thought it looked pretty good this time, now that my hair had been trimmed.

At least one thing was settled: Ashley and I might be Facebook friends, but we still weren't friends in real life.

The rest of the day was like a Lemony Snicket novel, a series of unfortunate events. First, Jean-Paul wasn't at school. Then, when we picked up Rosie at the daycare in the basement, she was sitting in the corner again. Alison, the daycare lady, approached me.

"Violet, could you ask your mother to call me, please?"

I watched as Phoebe made a beeline over to Rosie and scooped her up. "Why?"

"She bit Isabelle again."

"What happened?"

"They won't tell us. They were playing with the dollhouse. We heard Isabelle scream, and Rosie's teeth were clamped down on her arm."

"Isabelle must have said something to upset her," I said.

"Whatever Isabelle said," Alison replied slowly, like I was stupid, "biting is unacceptable."

On the way home, we got the story out of Rosie. "We were playing house, and Isabelle said I couldn't have a daddy doll because I don't have a daddy at home, and I said we do have a daddy, he just doesn't live with us, and she said that meant we don't really have a daddy. So I bit her."

"You know what, Rosie?" I said. "I would've bit her, too."

Then, when we stopped in at Mom's work, we found her comforting Amanda, who was in tears.

"What's wrong?" we asked in unison.

"Oh, it's nothing," Amanda said, even though that was obviously a lie. "Cosmo and I are just . . ."

My heart did a flip. I knew it was ridiculous, but even a cynic like me had to hold on to a small thread of hope that True Love might exist for a lucky few, and Amanda and Cosmo were the flame that kept my hope alive.

"Please tell me you didn't break up," I said, my voice a bit wobbly.

"No, no . . . but he's been acting strange lately. He canceled a date last night with the lousiest explanation . . . and when we do get together, it's like there's something he wants to tell me, but he can't bring himself to say it. Like he's got some big secret."

Phoebe and I looked at each other. Amanda must have been a mind reader because she said, "And don't you girls even *think* of spying on him. I mean it!"

Then she started crying again so Mom shooed us away, saying she'd see us at home later.

Rosie and I said good-bye to Phoebe at her house because she had her French horn lesson. When we got to our place, Mr. Bright was on his front porch. "Tell your mother to get that muffler of hers fixed, or I'll have to call the authorities!" he shouted. The muffler on the Rust Bucket had broken over the weekend and made a loud clanking sound whenever Mom drove it.

"I'll tell her, Mr. Bright," I said as I hurried Rosie into our house and locked the door.

The phone was ringing. I made a run for it, not bothering to take off my shoes. "Hello?" I said, grabbing it just before it went to voice mail.

"Violet, hi." A female voice. Not my mom's voice.

"Hi. Who's this?"

"It's Jennica."

My stomach lurched. Wife Number Two *never* phoned. She was The Other Woman. *Why on earth would she be calling?* Unless –

"Is Dad okay? Has something happened to him?" Rosie was standing beside me, and I instinctively grabbed her hand.

"No, no, your dad is fine," she said. "Terrific, in fact. He's just been hired to direct this big TV pilot for a new show called *Out There.* It's like a cross between *Lost* and *Touched by an Angel.* He'll be shooting on the Tantamount lot."

"Oh," I said. "Cool." I let go of Rosie's hand, and she dashed upstairs.

There was a really long pause after that. I was tempted to run and get the Magic 8 Ball and let it do the talking, but I couldn't put Jennica through that. The truth was, I still didn't know her all that well. It's much easier to be cruel to someone you know.

"Lola and Lucy ask after you and Rosie a lot," Jennica finally said.

"Do they?" I answered, although inside I was thinking *liar.*

"They know you're supposed to come down for March Break."

"I wanna go, I wanna go!" Rosie's voice suddenly came on the line. The little sneak was listening in on the phone in Mom's bedroom.

"Rosie, is that you?" Jennica asked.

"Hi, Jenny. How's Lola and Lucy?"

"They're great. Talking up a blue streak. And they miss their older sisters a lot."

"See, I told you they missed us, Violet," Rosie said smugly.

"Get off the phone, Rosie."

"No! Do you really want us to come, Jenny?"

"Of course."

"Even after what Violet did?"

"Well, that's partly why I'm calling. We still very much want you girls to visit us. But, Violet, I need two things from you first: I need you to promise you will never do something like that to your sisters again, and I need you to apologize."

I was quiet for a long time. Rosie was not. "Please, Violet, please please please say you're sorry. Mom won't let me fly on the plane without you."

"Rosie. Get. Off. The. Phone." She must have heard the tone in my voice because I heard a *click.*

"Why are you calling, and not Dad?" I asked.

"Because Ian says you won't talk to him when he calls. I told him I'd give it a try."

There was another long pause.

"So. What do you say, Violet?"

I closed my eyes. I took a deep breath. Then, very quietly, I hung up.

I climbed the stairs to our room. Rosie was on the floor, playing with her Playmobil grocery set.

"Are we going? Are we going for March Break?"

I picked the Magic 8 Ball up from the shelf and gave it a good shake. *"Outlook not so good."*

"Uh-huh. Yes . . . yes, I think we can both agree that it's not okay to bite. But it's also not okay to dump all the blame on Rosie every single time there's an incident with this girl. . . ." My mom was heating up a jar of spaghetti sauce on the stove while she spoke on the phone. I could tell she was agitated because she was stirring really hard. Sauce kept spraying out of the pot and landing on the stove top and on her shirt. Rosie and I busied ourselves setting the table while we listened in.

"Clearly this girl is provoking her. You need to talk to her, too. . . . Well, according to Rosie, she told her that her dad didn't count because he doesn't live with us. For heaven's sake, half the kids at the daycare must have divorced or single parents, this isn't the 1950s. . . ." Mom picked up the pot of noodles from the stove, turned off the heat, and drained it in the colander that Rosie liked to wear on her head.

"Okay. Thank you. And if you want me to come in for a meeting with the other girl's parents, I'm happy to do it . . . bye." She hit the *off* button on the phone. I could tell she was angry by the way she pursed her lips.

"Are you mad at me, Mommy?" Rosie asked as Mom dished spaghetti and sauce onto our plates.

Mom knelt down beside her. "I'm not happy that you keep biting this girl, Rosie. But I also understand that they're not getting both sides of the story. Honestly, these people are supposed to be trained in early childhood education."

We started to eat. I had suggested to Rosie that if she told Mom about the call from Jennica, one of her dolls might mysteriously lose its head. So I was rather impressed by her courage when she announced, "Daddy's new wife called today."

Mom dropped her fork. It clattered onto her plate. "Did she?" Mom asked, in an eerily calm voice.

"She says we're still invited to their house for March Break. But she wanted Violet to say sorry for the poop first. Please please, I wanna go; they got a pool."

Mom looked at me. "Did you apologize?"

"Not exactly."

"Not exactly?"

"I kind of hung up."

"Oh, Violet." She picked up her fork again.

I shrugged. "It doesn't matter. I don't want to go, anyway."

"That's beside the point."

"How so?"

"You have to maintain a relationship with your father."

"Why?"

"Because he's your *father.*"

"So? You were his wife, and you don't have to 'maintain a relationship.'"

"That's different and you know it. Besides, those girls are your sisters."

"Half sisters –"

"*Please,* Violet!" Rosie begged.

"No!" I shouted. "I hate going down there! I hate having to act like everything's okay. It's not okay! Jennica ruined our lives. Everything was perfect before she came along."

Mom put her fork down again. "Everything wasn't perfect, Violet. Your dad and I had been drifting apart for a while –"

I clamped my hands to my ears. *"La-la-la-la-la-la-la-la-la!"* I chanted, standing up so fast, I tipped over my chair. I couldn't pick it up without taking my hands away from my ears, so I left it there and took the stairs two at a time to my room. Okay, it was not the most mature reaction in the world, but, really, I wasn't going to listen to my mom as she tried to reinvent history.

I picked up Rosie's doll Roxanna from her bed, popped her head off, left her decapitated body lying on

Rosie's pillow, and hid the head in a shoe box at the back of the closet. Then I rearranged all of our clothes in order of the color spectrum, thoughts racing through my head.

They did not have problems. They had been perfectly, utterly happy.

Hadn't they?

— 14 —

My bad mood flowed right into Friday. Jean-Paul still wasn't at school. I got a *C* on my math test. It was raining cats and dogs on the way home, and I ruined my brown suede Converse shoes when I accidentally stepped into a giant puddle.

Once we were inside, I picked the mail up from the floor and had a quick look. There were two bills and one brown eight-by-ten envelope.

From Los Angeles. With a sticker in the top left corner that read *From the Office of George Clooney.*

My heart started to race.

"I'm hungry," said Rosie. "Can you make me a snack?"

"Get your own snack," I snapped. "I'm not your servant."

"You're a poop-head," Rosie said matter-of-factly before she tore off into the kitchen.

I could hardly breathe. Carefully I tore open the envelope and pulled out the letter inside.

Dear **Violet,**

Thank you for your fan letter to George Clooney. Unfortunately, due to the volume of fan mail he receives, we must respond with a form letter.

However, please be assured that George appreciates the time you took to write to him, and as an expression of his gratitude, we have enclosed a signed eight-by-ten glossy of him for your collection.

Sincerely,
The Office of George Clooney

"A form letter?" Phoebe said when I called her. "Violet, I'm so sorry."

"Rmph," I muttered. I was sprawled out on the red couch, beyond depressed.

"You know what I think? I think George never even saw your letter. I think his manager just handed it off to an assistant or something."

"You're probably right." I heard the key in the lock. "Mom's home. I'd better go."

"Right. The official Gustafson Girls' Night. Maybe that'll cheer you up," said Phoebe. "We'll strategize tomorrow."

I put down the phone, dragged myself off the couch, and shuffled into the foyer. "I hope you got a comedy," I said to my mom. "I could use some laughs –"

I stopped midsentence. Mom wasn't alone.

"Violet, I told Dudley he could join us for movie night. I hope you don't mind," she said. The Wiener shifted nervously from foot to foot beside her, clutching a bag of take-out food from Zipang.

"It's not called Movie Night. It's called *Girls'* Night," I said.

"Maybe I should just go –" Dudley began.

"No, stay!" shouted Rosie as she ran in from the kitchen with what looked like chocolate ice cream smeared all over her face. "I want you to stay. So does Mom." She looked at me hopefully. "So does Violet. Right, Violet?"

I just rolled my eyes.

"I brought you girls a box of Purdy's Chocolates," he said, holding it out to us. "Vanilla creams and caramels." Purdy's vanilla creams were my favorite. Purdy's caramels were Rosie's favorite. Obviously Mom had fed him this piece of intel. It was a blatant and pathetic attempt to win us over, and I refused to reach for the box. Not that it mattered since Rosie grabbed it out of his hands faster than you could say *pushover.*

"You can sit beside me for the movie," Rosie said to him.

"Speaking of movies," Dudley said as we went into

the living room with the food, "did you see the one about the cannibal who ate his mother-in-law? It was called *Gladiator.* Get it? Glad I ate her?"

Mom laughed. I gazed at him stonily. "Let me guess. Another yard-sale find?" I asked him, pointing at his hideous sweater. This one featured a mallard on the front.

"No. Someone made it for me. I like this sweater." He actually sounded hurt.

"It's a lovely sweater," Mom said, patting his arm. Then she turned to me. "I saw your math test on the hall table. You got a *C*."

I shrugged. "It was geometry. I hate geometry."

"Now, Violet," Dudley said, "without geometry, there'd be no point." He laughed at his own feeble pun. I did not. "Sorry, I forgot. You don't like puns. But that's okay. A good pun is its own *reword*."

It was going to be a long night.

Mom had rented *The Fantastic Mr. Fox.* Mr. Fox was voiced by George Clooney, which I knew Phoebe would find interesting from a psychological perspective.

"Mom met George Clooney once," I announced, when we heard his distinct voice for the first time.

"Really? You met George Clooney?" asked Dudley, clearly impressed.

"I met a lot of actors when I worked in production," my mom said. "But George was by far the sweetest. And the hottest."

"He said he hoped their paths would cross again," I added.

"George Clooney has good taste," Dudley replied, then he actually gave my mom a kiss on the lips, right in front of us. I had to force myself not to gag. "Actually, I get told quite often that I could be his twin," he joked, sticking out his nonexistent chin and giving us a cheesy smile. Mom laughed too hard, and Rosie laughed too, even though she had no idea what was funny.

"In your dreams," I said under my breath.

Throughout the movie, Dudley sat on the red couch, with my mom on one side and Rosie on the other. I sat as far away from them as possible on the gold couch, even though I could barely see the TV screen. It was a good movie, but I couldn't concentrate because, out of the corner of my eye, I could see both my mom *and* my sister leaning in to Dudley. He held my mom's hand throughout practically the whole film, like a lovesick teenager. Honestly, it was all very *ick*.

After the movie Mom brought out Pictionary, but I didn't want to play. I felt sick. Mom said it was the eight vanilla creams I'd eaten. I knew better.

So I went upstairs while the three of them played the game. I read one of the Cherub books, envying James and his sister Lauren, who were not only kid spies, but orphans too. After a while, Mom brought Rosie up to bed. I helped get her into a pair of pull-ups, and she fell asleep almost instantly. I got into my pajamas and lay awake for as long as I could, waiting to hear Dudley leave. I thought I heard the door open and shut around midnight, just before I fell into a deep sleep.

I woke around 3:00 a.m. with serious stomach cramps. I burped and it tasted like acid and vanilla, a truly nasty combination.

I stumbled out of bed and hurried down the hall to the bathroom. My eyes were only half-open, so I didn't see him till the last second. He was coming from the other direction, also heading to the bathroom.

Dudley.

Naked Dudley.

Well, almost naked – he was wearing underpants, *thank you, God.*

I screamed.

He screamed.

And I tried not to look, I really did, but his blinding white flesh was right there in front of me, and I couldn't help but notice his moobs, his flabby stomach, and his hairy legs, which were too skinny for the rest of his body.

Mom came running out of her bedroom, a robe wrapped around her.

"Omigod, Violet, I'm sorry. I should have told you Dudley might stay over."

"Violet, I – I –" Dudley stuttered.

I didn't wait to hear any more. I pushed past the two of them and went into the bathroom, locking the door behind me.

Then I proceeded to barf up every single one of those vanilla cream chocolates.

— 15 —

Thanks to the severe trauma I'd suffered, I didn't manage to fall back to sleep until 5:00 a.m. It was eleven the next morning when I finally woke up.

I got out of my pajamas and slipped on yesterday's clothes. I didn't want to go downstairs. Even though I was pretty sure The Wiener would be long gone by now, I knew I was destined for one of Mom's talks.

I was half-right. When I got downstairs, I found Rosie in the living room, snuggled up to Dudley while he read her *Stanley's Party*, one of her favorite books. I couldn't even look at him.

"Where's Mom?"

"She's having a shower," Dudley replied, and he blushed.

Good, I thought. *You should be embarrassed! You should also buy some new underpants and a gym membership!*

"Rosie, where's Mom?" I asked, ignoring Dudley.

"Dudley just said. She's having a shower." Then she looked up at Dudley with big adoring eyes. "Keep reading."

"You can read later, Rosie. Let's go to Liberty Bakery and get some treats."

"Too late. Me and Dudley already went," she replied.

My insides felt sour. "But I always go with you."

"You was sleeping," she said simply.

"We brought you back a monster-sized scone. And Ingrid made a big fruit salad. I'll get a plate ready for you," said Dudley, starting to get up.

"I'm not hungry," I said, even though my stomach was growling loud enough for them to hear.

"I wanted to mention . . ." Dudley continued, and for one horrified moment, I thought he was going to bring up the traumatizing events of last night, ". . . if you ever need help with your math homework, I'm a bit of a whiz. . . ."

I gave him the hairy eyeball, which shut him up. Mom entered the living room a moment later, dressed for the day, her hair freshly washed.

"Good. You're up. Why don't you come into the kitchen with me for a moment?"

Sigh.

I shuffled into the kitchen behind her. Mom poured herself a cup of coffee. I leaned against the counter.

"I want to apologize again, Violet. I should have told you Dudley might stay over."

"Yes. You should have."

"The truth is, it took us by surprise, too."

Ew. "Yeah, well. Don't let it happen again," I said.

There was a pause. "I can't promise that –"

Suddenly a sound reverberated through the house – a sound I hadn't heard in over a year.

"The doorbell's working," I said.

My mom smiled. "Dudley fixed it this morning."

From where I stood, I could see Dudley as he answered the door. *Our* door. It was some guy from Greenpeace, and Dudley started chatting to him about climate change. Rosie ran to join him. She leaned into him and wrapped her little arms around his leg, as if she was afraid that if she didn't, he'd leave and never come back.

"He's going to fix the washing machine next," Mom continued. "Apparently it just needs a new thingamajig. We won't have to do laundry at Phoebe's anymore."

"We?"

"You know what I meant –"

"Nobody asked him to fix our doorbell."

Mom took a deep breath. "You're right. He just went ahead and did it while I was making coffee."

"He should have asked first."

"Violet –"

"It's not his doorbell! It's our doorbell!" I felt tears pricking my eyes, and I hated myself for it. I jumped up and ran out of the kitchen, pushing past Dudley, Rosie, and the Greenpeace guy at the door.

"You're not wearing shoes!" Rosie shouted after me.

I didn't care. All I could see was black. I felt like I wanted to punch something or someone. I felt like I wanted to scream at the top of my lungs.

At Phoebe's house, Günter opened the front door. He took in my T-shirt and bare feet. "I'll get you some slippers" was all he said as he pulled me into their house.

"You saw him *naked*?"

"Not totally, thank God. He was wearing underpants."

We were sitting in Phoebe's bedroom. Günter had brought me a bowl of porridge, which I was devouring.

"What kind?"

"Briefs. Old ones. They were all saggy in the bum." I shuddered at the memory. "He probably gets his underwear at yard sales, too."

"So, they must have, you know, *dot dot dot* . . ."

"Duh."

I slurped up the last of the brown-sugar-flavored

milk from my porridge bowl. "You know the weird part?" I continued. "The *dot dot dot* doesn't bug me as much as the doorbell. The doorbell makes me crazy."

"That's because it's not about the doorbell," Phoebe said. "It's about what the doorbell represents. If your dad was still living with you, *he* would have fixed the doorbell, right? That sort of stuff was his territory, as man of the house."

"I guess so, yeah."

"So by fixing your doorbell, Dudley's acting like *he's* the man of the house. It's like he's auditioning to become your father's replacement."

I groaned; it was worse than I thought. "And Mom and Rosie are falling for it."

"You really dislike him, huh?"

"There's just something about him, Phoebe. He's always this jokey kind of guy . . . but it's like there's something darker lurking underneath."

Phoebe thought for a moment. "Okay, then. Here's what we need to do. One, more detective work. And two," she grabbed her laptop from under a pile of dirty socks on the floor, "you need to write another letter to George Clooney. And write one to his manager while you're at it."

This is what I wrote.

Dear Sir:

I sent your client, George Clooney, a letter a few weeks ago. Yesterday I received a form letter in response. I won't lie: That hurt.

It also made me suspect that you, Sir, are not actually giving him his mail. I am positive that if George had actually read my letter, he would have responded. Don't deny it; I'm on to you.

George deserves to read his own letters. He is not a child. Remember: You work for George. George does not work for you.

I am enclosing a copy of the letter I sent on January 19 in the hopes that this time, Sir, you will do the right thing and give my letter to the man it was intended for.

Thank you in advance,

Violet Gustafson

Dear Mr. Clooney,

Hello again. It's me, Violet Gustafson, Ingrid's daughter. I hope that by the time you read this, your manager has done the right thing and passed on the letter I sent you almost a month ago (I'll enclose another copy just in case). You should really have a talk with him, George. I don't have actual physical proof, but I'm almost positive he's reading your mail and not even giving you a chance to see it. Maybe it's time for a new manager.

(George's manager, if you are reading this right now, STOP. Take a long look at yourself in the mirror and DO THE RIGHT THING.)

Anyway, George – please *read my letter. If you detect a note of urgency in my tone this time, you would be correct. See, last time I wrote, my mom had just started dating this guy named Dudley Wiener (yes, it's his real name). I didn't bother mentioning him because, to be honest, I figured he'd be like the dinosaurs by now, i.e., ancient history.*

But he isn't, George. It's over a month later and he's still very much in the picture. Trust me when I say she deserves so much better. So please – don't wait a moment longer. Respond to my letter ASAP.

With anticipation and appreciation,

Violet Gustafson

Phoebe and I printed the letters and put them into two separate envelopes. We walked to the corner and put them into the mailbox. Then we went back to her place to eat bagels and cream cheese from Solly's and strategize about our next stakeout.

WHEN: *Next Saturday.*

WHERE: *Dudley's house.*

OBJECTIVE: *If The Wiener has a skeleton in his closet, we will find it.*

— 16 —

"You're right. Detective work can be kind of boring," Jean-Paul said to me on Saturday morning, as we crouched together behind the newspaper box at Main and Eleventh. Phoebe was in Skip to My Loo across the street.

That's right. Jean-Paul was with us. I still couldn't believe it.

What happened was this: He'd finally showed up at school on Tuesday morning. When Phoebe and I walked past his locker, I said, aiming for casual, "Oh, hey, Jean-Paul. Where have you been?"

"My dad flew me to Winnipeg for a long weekend."

"How was it?"

"Great," he said. "We played hockey on the outdoor rink every day. And he took me to Ray and Jerry's. It's this awesome steak house. Mom hardly ever cooks red meat, so I stuffed myself."

"Sounds fun," I said. I was about to walk away, but Phoebe grabbed my arm, forcing me to stay.

"We're going on another stakeout this Saturday," she told him.

"Cool. Can I come?"

"Well, it won't be very interesting," I started.

"Of course you can come," Phoebe said.

Jean-Paul smiled. "Great. You can give me the details later. See you in class."

Then he walked away. Phoebe just looked at me and shook her head. "Honestly, Violet. What would you do without me?"

"I've often asked myself the same question."

Phoebe, Jean-Paul, and I had met up at 9:00 a.m. sharp at the corner of Main and King Edward. First we'd headed to The Wiener's apartment, which wasn't far from his shop. I'd realized on Friday that I didn't actually know where he lived, and I agonized over how to ask my mom for his address without raising suspicion. But, as usual, Phoebe saved the day: She just looked him up in the online white pages. He was, not surprisingly, the only "D. Wiener" listed.

The building Dudley lived in was a bit shabby. His apartment was on the second floor, and the windows were spotted with rain. Through our binoculars, we could make out only a few things: shelves overflowing with books; a floral-patterned couch that seemed an odd choice for a man; a fish tank; and a dying fern. At one point, I tried to sneak into the building behind a little old lady, but she gave me the hairy eyeball and closed the door in my face. Twenty minutes after that, Dudley stepped out, dressed for work. We'd followed him, staying about a block behind. Aside from buying a muffin and a coffee at Bean Around the World, he didn't make any stops before reaching his shop. Phoebe waited for a good ten minutes after he'd turned the CLOSED sign to OPEN before she crossed the street.

"That's a unique toque," Jean-Paul said to me.

"I'll pretend that was a compliment," I replied. I was wearing the beagle toque Amanda had made me for Christmas.

"Anyway, look who's talking," I said, "you're dressed for a stakeout in Siberia."

He laughed. "You're right! This is how we dress for winter in Winnipeg." He was wearing a down-filled parka with a big fake-fur-lined hood. When he had it up, he had no peripheral vision. On his feet was a big pair of Sorel winter boots. "But at least I'm warm. How are you?"

"Fine." That was a lie. It was a cold, damp, drizzly March day, and despite having two layers of fleece under my rain jacket and a pair of long johns under my jeans, I was shivering.

"Your nose is red," Jean-Paul said. He pulled off a mitten and touched the tip of it with his finger. "And freezing."

Body contact. I felt tingly all over. The monologue going on inside my head was deafening.

This is the moment. This is your chance to invite him to the Sadie Hawkins Dance.

(But I don't want to go to the dance! I don't believe in this sort of stuff!)

Liar! You're totally in love with him!

(You're the liar. I am not in love. Love is –)

Nothing but trouble, blah blah blah. Shut up and ask him!

Honestly, it was not pleasant. But I couldn't shut it off.

I opened my mouth to respond – then I saw him wipe his hand on his jeans before he slid his mitten back on. The inner monologue started up again.

Oh, God. Is my nose running? Did his finger come away wet? Gross! I can't ask him to the dance moments after he's touched my snot!

As my inner voice continued to torment me, Phoebe bounced up beside us. "Nothing interesting, sorry," she said, grabbing my backpack and pulling out a sandwich. We'd told our parents we were going to the library to work on a school project, so the pack was filled with decoy books as well as food.

"I'll go in for a while," said Jean-Paul.

Then he did the most amazing thing. He took off his parka and wrapped it around my shoulders. "Here, wear it while I'm gone. It'll warm you up in no time."

I pulled the parka close as he headed across the street, breathing in his scent.

"Did you do it?" Phoebe demanded. "Did you invite him to the dance?"

I shook my head. Phoebe had invited Andrew at school the day before, and he'd said yes.

"But the dance is on Wednesday, Violet."

"I know, I know. I tried. But I'm very conflicted –"

"Violet, seriously. This is getting tired. It's obvious you like him. So take the plunge! Take a chance on romance. Be like the Nike ad: Just Do It!"

"Okay, okay, enough."

Phoebe and I ate more sandwiches while we waited for Jean-Paul. His coat was luxuriously warm. Within ten minutes, I was completely toasty. After twenty minutes, I wanted to have a nap.

I was stifling a huge yawn when we saw Jean-Paul leave the store. He walked across the street, then he strolled right past us, motioning for us to follow him.

He ducked around a corner. We gathered up all of our gear, and, after making sure Dudley wasn't looking out the window, we joined him.

"You won't believe this," he told us. "I went in and started to browse. He remembered me. He asked if my mom liked the soap. Then the phone rang. He went behind the counter to answer the call. It must have been a friend or someone he knew."

"Male or female?"

"I don't know. But I heard him say, *I can't tonight. I already have plans.*"

"That's right," I said. "He's coming to our place for a dinner party. My mom thinks it's time he met her friends."

"Then the friend must have asked about Sunday because he said, *Sunday's no good either, I'm afraid. I'm going to see my wife.*"

— 17 —

"Going to see my wife* could mean a lot of things," Phoebe reasoned, as the three of us trudged back up Main Street.

"It could mean she's in the hospital," said Jean-Paul. "Or a mental institution."

"Or it could mean they're separated and are still trying to work things out," Phoebe said.

"Or it could mean they're married, and he's going to pick her up at the airport," I said. "No matter how you slice it, it's not good."

"You're right, Violet," Phoebe said. "You thought he had a secret, and he does."

I should have felt triumphant, but to tell the truth, I felt kind of glum. *What would it do to my mom to find out that Dudley was just one more jerk to add to the jerk pile?*

We reached Jean-Paul's street and stood for a moment on the sidewalk in the drizzle.

"What are you going to do?" asked Jean-Paul.

Phoebe and I looked at each other. "Well, he is coming for dinner tonight," I said.

"Careful," Phoebe cautioned. "Remember Jonathan."

"Jonathan got what he deserved."

"All I'm saying is, don't make a scene," Phoebe said. "Be a little more subtle."

I nodded. "I can do subtle."

Three hours later, our house started to fill up with guests. The first person to arrive was The Wiener. He was wearing his hideous mallard sweater again.

He handed my mom a bottle of wine. "Homemade," he said, like this was a good thing. Then he handed Rosie and me small bottles of pink stuff. "It's peppermint foot cream," he told us. "You'd be a *heel* not to like it."

Mom laughed. "Dudley, you're such a goof."

I tossed my cream onto the hall table.

"Violet, aren't you going to introduce Phoebe?" Mom asked.

"Oh. Sure. This is Phoebe, my best friend," I said, indicating Phoebe, who was standing in the entranceway to the living room.

"Pleased to meet you," Phoebe said.

Dudley shook her hand. "You look familiar," he said to her. "You were in my shop today, weren't you? Skip to My Loo? On Main?"

Mom shot Phoebe and me a look.

"I was studying today," Phoebe lied. "Perhaps it was my evil twin."

The doorbell rang again, saving us from further questions. Cathy and Günter stood on the front porch. "The bell's working," Cathy exclaimed as they entered. Behind them, Amanda and Cosmo were making their way up the walk. They were holding hands and giggling, not looking at all like a couple who were having problems. Karen tottered in on her high heels a moment later.

The front hall was filled with bodies as people took off their coats and handed over food and bottles of wine. Mom introduced everyone to Dudley, and they all tried to look like they weren't checking him out in a big way. I could see beads of sweat forming on his freckled forehead, and, for a moment, I almost felt sorry for him.

Until I remembered his wife.

"Hey, Violet," Karen said as we made our way into the living room, "do you know a girl named Ashley Anderson?"

Phoebe and I shared a look. "She's a girl in my class. Why?"

"I had a *friend request* from her on Facebook. We have one friend in common, and it's you."

Ew. There was something creepy about knowing that Ashley had viewed my friends list. *And why would she try to "friend" one of them – someone she didn't even know?* "You didn't friend her back."

"Sure I did."

"But you don't even know her!"

"So? I broke the three hundred mark. Now my goal is four hundred friends! Besides, what harm can it do?"

I shook my head. Karen was an idiot. But on the other hand, she had a point: What harm could it do?

After the adults had a predinner drink, Dudley helped Mom add the leaves to the dining table. Phoebe, Rosie, and I brought up extra folding chairs from the basement. Soon we were all sitting around the table eating my mom's roasted lemon chicken, along with Amanda's Caesar salad, Günter's roasted vegetables, and Karen's store-bought bread. The adults, minus Cosmo, drank a lot of wine. Phoebe and I kept kicking each other under the table as we watched one of Cosmo's tattoos move on his biceps while he ate.

"Ingrid, this chicken is *poultry* in motion," Dudley said.

A few of the adults groaned. *See?* I wanted to shout. *This is what I've had to put up with!*

"Dudley's a bit of a punster," my mom said.

"*Lettuce* not forget Amanda's salad," said Cosmo with a grin.

"And the roasted vegetables are *parsnip-ularly* delicious," Cathy added. "I *yam* very impressed."

Traitors, I thought.

Cosmo started tapping the side of his water glass. "Since we're all gathered here tonight, Amanda and I have some news." The table went quiet. "I've asked Amanda to marry me."

"And I've said yes," Amanda said.

The room burst into spontaneous applause. Rosie leapt up and crawled onto Amanda's lap and kissed her cheeks, then she kissed Cosmo's cheeks, too, and everyone laughed.

I was so happy, I felt tears spring to my eyes. Then just as quickly, I was hit by a wave of anxiety. *What if it didn't work out?*

"Ingrid, I'd like you to be my maid of honor."

"Absolutely."

"Karen, would you be one of my bridesmaids?"

Karen shrugged. "Story of my life. Always the bridesmaid, never the bride." Then she grabbed Amanda's hand. "I'd love to."

"Who's going to be your best man?" Phoebe asked Cosmo.

"A kid named Ambrose. He's my downstairs neighbor, and he's the reason Amanda and I met each other."

"You know how I told you Cosmo canceled a date on me recently? He was picking out a ring with his mother," Amanda said. "And those times when it seemed like he wanted to tell me something –"

"I was getting up the nerve to propose. I was terrified you'd say no," he said.

Karen sighed heavily and knocked back the rest of her wine. "Where can I find a guy like you, Cosmo? Or like you, Dudley, or you, Günter?"

"Not at the clubs you hang out at, that's for sure," said Mom, and everyone laughed, even Karen.

I couldn't take my eyes off Amanda and Cosmo. They looked so unbelievably happy, it made my heart hurt. And then I remembered that Mom and Dad had probably looked that happy, too, when they'd decided to tie the knot.

"Kind of funny when you think about it," I heard myself saying. "You two are *getting* married; my mom *was* married; and Dudley *is* married."

Dead silence. Phoebe kicked my shin under the table. Hard.

"What on earth are you talking about?" my mom said.

My body was shaking, but I could hardly stop now. "A friend of mine just happened to be in your store today," I said, looking directly at Dudley, "and he overheard you on the phone. You said you were going to visit your wife tomorrow."

Dudley put down his fork. My mom put her head in her hands.

"Violet," my mom said, "I'm going with Dudley tomorrow. And I've gone with him before."

My head was spinning. "You've met his wife? You're having an *affair* with a married man? Didn't you learn your lesson with Larry the Unibrow?"

"My wife is dead, Violet," Dudley said quietly. "I go to visit her gravesite once a month."

Oh.

Amanda finally broke the silence. "I'm so sorry, Dudley."

"Yeah, man, that's rough," Cosmo added.

"Do you mind telling us . . . ?" Karen began.

"Not at all. It was ovarian cancer. She died five years ago."

Rosie climbed off Amanda's lap and hurried around the table to crawl onto Dudley's. "That's sad," she said to him, as she gently stroked his cheek.

"Yes, it is," he replied, and he looked like he was going to cry. My mom laid her hand on his shoulder. "She was a knitter too, you know," he said to Amanda. "She knit almost all my sweaters, including the one I'm wearing. It's my favorite."

Great.

No one glanced my way, except for Phoebe, who sat on my left. "Smooth. Like butter," she murmured.

I waited for my mom to shout at me or send me to my room. But she didn't. She didn't even look at me. "But back to the good news. I'd like to raise a toast to Amanda and Cosmo. You make a wonderful couple, and I wish you great happiness together." She raised her wineglass.

"Cheers!" everyone shouted.

I just sat very still in my chair. When people stood up to clear away dishes, I slipped upstairs to my room.

I half-expected my mom to follow me and give me a big lecture, but she didn't. No one came up, except for Phoebe. She knocked on my door a few minutes later and handed me a piece of cake. "That was your idea of subtle?"

I just dipped my finger into the icing.

Phoebe sat across from me on Rosie's bed. "Violet, I have to say something, and you're probably not going to like it."

"Then don't say it."

"You want your mom to be happy, right?"

"Duh."

"So, maybe Dudley makes her happy. I mean, now that I've seen him and your mom together . . . he's not a bad guy. He's easygoing. He's funny in a dorky, old-fashioned kind of way. And he's almost cute, if you look at him in the right light –"

I slammed my hands over my ears. *"La-la-la-la-la-la-la-la-la!"*

Phoebe stared at me till I stopped. "Very mature. I'm just giving it to you straight, Violet."

"Well, don't." I could feel tears well up in my eyes. "You're supposed to be my best friend."

"I *am* your best friend. Would you rather I be like Lauren and just say whatever you want to hear?"

"Right now, yes! Your parents are together. They're happy. You have no idea what it's like."

"I do know what it's like. I hear it from you every day!"

"Well, I'm sorry to bore you. I won't anymore."

"Now you're being an idiot."

"Leave me alone."

"Violet –"

"Seriously. Get out."

Phoebe stared at me for a moment. Then she marched out of my room and slammed the door.

I had never fought with Phoebe before.

After she left, I locked myself in the upstairs bathroom and rearranged all the items under the sink, from largest to smallest. Then I rearranged them again, from smallest to largest. Then I cried a little. Then I went back to my bedroom and crawled into bed and fell into a deep, dreamless sleep.

— 18 —

All was quiet when I woke up the next morning at ten. Rosie wasn't in her bed. Eventually I forced myself to get up and tiptoed down to the kitchen.

The house was empty. For a moment I was filled with panic, and a pile of irrational thoughts raced through my head: Aliens had taken Mom and Rosie in the middle of the night; Dudley was really a mass murderer, who'd killed them and stuffed the bodies somewhere; or, and in some ways this was the worst thought of all, they'd just got so fed up with me that they'd packed their bags and left to build a new life somewhere else.

Before I could get to a full-on panic, I found the note on the kitchen table.

Gone to cemetery with Rosie and Dudley.
Might check out some yard sales afterward.
Back later this aft. I have my cell. Love, Mom.

The word "love" filled me with relief.

I ate a bowl of cereal, then I rearranged all the food in the cupboards according to food group. Afterward I went upstairs and washed my hair, twice.

I didn't know what to do with myself. Normally I'd call Phoebe, and we'd rehash the evening in minute detail, but for the first time in seven years, we weren't speaking.

I spent the afternoon in my bedroom, reading *The Pigman* and eating beef jerky from an enormous Costco bag.

I heard a car pull up around three. I didn't have to look out the window to know it was the Rust Bucket, since the muffler was still broken and you could hear it coming from a mile away.

I braced myself for a lecture. Sure enough, two minutes later there was a knock on my door. I didn't answer. Eventually the door opened, like I knew it would.

But it wasn't Mom. It was Dudley.

"Can I come in?"

No. "Free country," I said.

Dudley perched on Rosie's bed. He had to duck so his head wouldn't hit the sloped ceiling. "I just want to say, I'm not angry about last night. Or about the fact that you've been spying on me. I knew I'd seen your friend Phoebe before."

Silence.

"Your mom, on the other hand . . . she's pretty upset. So I asked her if I could speak to you instead." He clasped his hands together. "I rather admire you, Violet. I know you're just trying to protect your mom and your sister. But I also want you to know, I really care about Ingrid. And as long as she'll have me, I plan on sticking around. So I'm hoping you and I can call a truce."

He held out his hand. It took me a moment to realize he was waiting for me to shake it.

I picked up my Magic 8 Ball instead and gave it a good shake.

"Don't count on it."

His shoulders drooped. He stood up, forgetting about the sloped ceiling, hit his head, and left.

I didn't want to go downstairs, so for the rest of the afternoon and evening I survived on beef jerky and tap water, and the combo gave me wickedly smelly farts.

When I heard Mom climbing the stairs with Rosie to put her to bed, I flipped off my light and pretended to be asleep.

"She's not really asleep," I heard Rosie whisper. "She's pretending."

"It's a good thing," my mom replied, not making

any attempt to whisper, "because if she *was* awake, I'd have to kill her."

Nice.

"Not really though, right, Mommy?"

"Right." I heard her give Rosie a kiss. "Good night, Rosie."

Then, to my surprise, I felt her lips on my forehead, too.

"Good night, Violet."

— 19 —

Rosie was very pleased with herself as we walked to school on Monday. "My pull-ups were dry *again* this morning! That's three mornings in a row."

"That's great, Rosie," I mumbled.

We were walking past Phoebe's house. "Aren't we gonna pick her up?" asked Rosie.

"Not today."

"Daddy called yesterday morning," Rosie said. "He told me he could still get us plane tickets for March Break. All you need to do is say sorry."

I didn't answer.

Once I'd dropped Rosie at kindergarten, I made my way slowly up the stairs. Jean-Paul was at his locker. I stopped at the water fountain and had a drink, trying to focus my thoughts. The Sadie Hawkins Dance was only two nights away. And Phoebe was right: I *did* want to go with him, no matter how much I denied it.

"Hey, *Pamplemousse.*"

I jumped up, almost losing a tooth on the fountain.

"How did things go on Saturday night?"

"Terrible," I confessed. "Dudley's wife died a few years ago. He was going to visit her at the cemetery."

He frowned. "That's awful. I never would have thought of that."

"Me, neither."

We didn't say anything for a moment. And then, in what seemed to be the story of my life, I just blurted it out. "The Sadie Hawkins thingy this Wednesday, I thought – maybe – if you aren't busy – we could go. Together."

The words seemed to hang in the air between us.

"Wow," he said finally. "The thing is . . . Ashley called me last night and invited me. I thought – I mean, I didn't think you were going to – I said yes."

Oh.

"Sorry, *Pamplemousse.*"

I tried to smile. "Hey, no biggie. I didn't really want to go, anyway. I hate dances. Oh, is that the time? I'd better run."

I fled toward the classroom. *Oh, well,* I thought, *at least the day can't get any worse.*

I was so, so wrong.

As I neared our class, I heard laughter, which was unusual. Normally there was nothing to laugh about at school on a Monday morning.

A bunch of kids were gathered around our sole computer terminal at the back of the class. Ashley was in the middle, showing them something on the screen.

"Oh my God!" I heard one girl say.

"Ouch," said Claudia.

Lauren turned away from the computer screen for a moment. Our eyes met. She smirked and tapped Ashley on the shoulder. Ashley turned around.

"Violet, you poor thing!" Ashley said, her voice dripping with false concern. "Have you seen these photos on Facebook? Your mom's friend Karen posted them on the weekend."

It felt like I was walking in slow motion as I made my way toward the computer.

I looked at the screen.

The photos were almost a year old. In one, Mom and Karen were in crop-tops, their midriffs showing, drinking shooters. In another, they were drinking more shooters, and two guys had their arms around them. I recognized the guy who had his arm around my mom. It was Carl, the alcoholic.

But the worst photo showed my mom bending over Carl to kiss him. The top of her red thong underwear was clearly visible in her low-cut jeans.

I felt like I was underwater. I could see my classmates' faces – some laughing, some feeling sorry for me – but I couldn't hear anything. Jean-Paul stood near the doorway. Phoebe was nowhere to be seen.

I turned back and looked at Ashley. Suddenly I crashed to the surface again and could hear her shrieking with laughter. "You poor thing, Violet! I mean, irregardless of these photos –"

"Regardless," I said quietly.

"What?"

"It's *regardless. Irregardless* doesn't make sense. It's a double negative," I said, louder this time. "Anyone with half a brain knows that."

Her features hardened. "*Irregardless* of those photos, Pancake," she said, her voice like ice, "your mom is a total skank."

I had never swung a punch before in my life. But I guess there's a first time for everything.

— 20 —

FOR THE RECORD: I did not mean to break Thing One's nose.

I *did* mean to hit her, but I *didn't* mean to break anything. Not that the subtle difference mattered to Mr. Patil. When he entered the classroom, he saw Ashley clutching her nose, blood spurting between her fingers, and me, rubbing my sore knuckles. He marched me to the principal's office. And because I couldn't bring myself to tell the principal about the photos of my mother, I took all the blame.

"Mr. Patil will go with you while you gather up your things from your locker," Ms. Marlatt told me. "You're suspended for the rest of the week." Then she picked up the phone and called my mom at work.

Mom picked me up in the Rust Bucket twenty minutes

later. She was so upset, she didn't say a word, which was probably a good thing since I wouldn't have heard her over the noise of the busted muffler. When we arrived home, Mr. and Mrs. Bright were in their front yard, doing their first bit of spring gardening. They glared at Mom.

"You need to get that muffler fixed," Mr. Bright shouted.

"And you need to get your nose out of my business!" my mom shouted back, as she marched up the front steps and into the house.

The moment we were through the front door, she lit into me.

"Suspended! For the rest of the week!" She threw her car keys down on the entranceway table. "What is wrong with you these days, Violet? I don't even know who you are anymore! You're belligerent and rude. . . . You spy on my boyfriend. . . . You break a girl's nose! What has happened to you?"

"What's happened to *me*? What's happened to *you*?" I screamed back. "Do you know why I punched her, Mom? Because she called you a skank, that's why!"

Mom looked completely taken aback. "What are you talking about?"

"Your stupid friend Karen posted a bunch of her stupid photos on stupid Facebook. You're drinking in the photos. You're kissing Carl. You're showing off your thong underwear!"

All the color drained from Mom's face. "I can't believe Karen posted those pictures."

"I can't believe you were *in* those pictures!"

"Those pictures – it feels like a lifetime ago. It was a terrible time for me, Violet. I was depressed, I felt totally undesirable – I made some really stupid choices."

"Ever since Dad left, you've been this totally different person. Dressing like a teenager. Dating all these gross guys. Leaving *me* to do all the stuff you used to do – cooking dinner, doing the laundry, putting Rosie to bed –"

"You're right, Violet. None of this has been fair to you. But things are getting better. Now that Dudley –"

"Oh, please! Mom, he is so second-rate. You're only falling for him because you're desperate to have a man in your life!"

Mom looked like I'd just punched *her* in the nose.

"I need to get back to work," she said slowly. "I'm giving the students an exam this afternoon." She picked up her keys and walked toward the door.

I was thinking that I'd now managed to alienate pretty much every single person I'd ever cared about, when she turned back.

"I wasn't going to tell you yet, but last night, after you and Rosie went to bed, Dudley asked me to marry him." She walked out the door.

I stood there, frozen, listening to the Rust Bucket rattle and bang as Mom drove away.

I felt numb. I climbed the stairs and poured myself a scalding hot bath. I forced myself into it, grabbing the latest edition of *Entertainment Weekly* from the stand near the toilet. I was thinking that this wasn't one of the worst days in my life, it actually was *the* worst day of my life, right up there with the day Dad left, when something in the magazine caught my eye.

> **"British director Alfred Billingham started production yesterday on his new film, *Inside Job*. The movie is shooting at Tantamount Studios. George Clooney stars."**

Tantamount Studios. My mind started to race. *Why did it sound so familiar?* Then it hit me: Jennica had said Dad was shooting his new pilot at Tantamount Studios. George Clooney and my dad were working at the same studio.

I leapt out of the tub and called Dad on his cell phone, still dripping wet.

"Dad? It's Violet. I'm really sorry I fed cat turds to Lola and Lucy. And I really want to come to L.A."

— 21 —

"Cannonball!" Rosie shouted, before she launched her compact little body into the pool. She wore a brand-new swimsuit, one of those with a built-in flotation device. It was royal blue with dolphins on it, a gift from Wife Number Two when we'd arrived, just a few hours ago. Lucy and Lola were in the shallow end with Jennica, who wore a string bikini that showed off her tanned, curvy figure, and their part-time nanny, Anna Maria. The twins shrieked with delight, and I could tell that Rosie was loving being the cool older sibling for once.

As for me, I sat on a lounge chair in khaki cargo pants and a white T-shirt, blocking my face from the sun with a pair of Jennica's sunglasses and a floppy straw hat. I clutched one of the books I'd brought with me, *The Outsiders* by S.E. Hinton. The irony of the title was not lost on me. But I found it hard to concentrate on the story as sweat trickled down my front and pooled at the base of my training bra. The water looked cool, silky, and inviting, but I wasn't going near it today.

My mom must have told my dad that both of us needed new bathing suits because Jennica had bought me a new one, too. A bikini. With little cups where my boobs were supposed to go. I'd tried it on to be polite, and as I'd gazed at myself in the full-length mirror in the little change house beside the pool, I felt like the most tragic girl on the face of the earth. The bikini bottom sagged around my flat bony butt, and the top hung sadly with nothing to hold it up. I poked one of the cups with my finger, and it created a big concave indentation, which would have been funny if it didn't make me want to cry.

How could I have thought for a moment that Jean-Paul could be interested in me when he has Ashley falling all over him? Ashley might be a bitch, but she's a pretty bitch. I, on the other hand, am painfully average. Possibly even below average. I should have stuck to my vow.

I was starting to feel seriously sorry for myself when Jennica walked right into the change room without knocking.

"How does it fit?" she asked, before she had a chance to actually look at me and figure it out for herself. "Oh. No worries, the shop has a million different styles, and I know at least a dozen more that will look gorgeous on you." She smiled her trademark smile, showing off two rows of dazzling white teeth. "In the meantime, you can swim in your underwear if you want; it's just us girls."

Was she kidding me? "Thanks, but I'm actually feeling a bit chilled," I lied.

So here I was, sweltering under the hot sun instead. Rosie was showing the twins her dive, which looked more like a belly flop.

I got up and moved my chair into the shade. I polished off my Diet Coke and put the can beside my lounge chair. Jennica buys Diet Coke by the case, and since Mom doesn't buy pop except on special occasions, I drank a lot of it here. I belched softly and tried once again to read my book.

It had been just two days since I'd apologized to Dad on the phone, but once I'd done so, things moved really quickly. First, my mom had a long talk with my dad. "She's suspended. For the rest of the week." I could hear her through the vent in the bathroom, where I was brushing my teeth. "She punched a girl in the nose."

I noticed she didn't bring up the Facebook photos.

There was a long pause while she listened to my dad. "Don't you *dare* call my parenting skills into question, Ian, don't you dare. When is the last time you parented your daughters?"

I couldn't help it – I grinned. I love it when Mom tears a strip off Dad. It doesn't happen very often because they rarely speak, but it's awesome when it does.

"You need to take her off my hands for a while. I can barely cope with her these days."

My smile disappeared.

A couple of hours later, Mom announced that Jennica had found a last-minute deal for a flight leaving Wednesday morning. Rosie was delighted, especially since it meant she got to miss three days of daycare. We would be staying with them for ten days, our longest visit yet.

Mom and I barely spoke to each other when she drove us to the airport.

"Have a wonderful time," she said to Rosie as she showered her with kisses outside the security gate. Then she straightened up and looked at me. "Behave yourself," she said, before quickly kissing my forehead.

"What did you say to Dudley?" I asked.

She pursed her lips. "Nothing. I haven't answered him yet."

"Answered him about what?" Rosie piped up.

"Well, just – don't answer him," I pleaded. "Not until we're back."

She just grabbed us and hugged us. "Good-bye, my girls."

Then I'd taken Rosie's hand and the two of us went through the security gate. Three hours later, we'd landed in Los Angeles.

I gave up on my book and put it down beside the lounge chair. I looked around at the pool, the swing set, and the infamous sandbox. A stone fence surrounded the yard, just high enough so that you couldn't see the neighbors, and some sort of ivy fell from the stones.

Their home was beautiful. And I couldn't help it, my mind wandered to that place again, the place that fantasized about what our lives would be like if Dad hadn't met Jennica. We might have all moved down to L.A. and lived in a house with a pool. Mom probably would have insisted on a more modest house, and she wouldn't have hired a nanny, or decorated in the same way, or had as many clothes in the closet, but still. We'd have a pool instead of a rusted trampoline, and Rosie would have more toys and wouldn't have to wear my hand-me-downs. Maybe I would have my own room, and Mom would drive a nicer car, and our house wouldn't be falling apart.

Suddenly one of the twins toddled up to me. I could tell it was Lucy because her swimsuit was green. She hollered, "Up, up!" I pulled her onto my lap and hugged her. She was wet, but it felt good because I was so hot.

She didn't seem to remember that I was the wicked half sister who'd made her eat poo. Or, if she did remember, she didn't hold it against me. Pretty soon Lola, in her purple swimsuit, joined us, and I had both of them on my lap. As I held them tight, I realized I was crying. Tears were gushing down my face, hot tears of shame for what I had done to these two little girls, who'd never, ever done anything to hurt me except to be born.

Next thing I knew, Rosie was slapping her way over, a pair of flippers on her feet. She frowned at me through her blue-green goggles, her arms crossed over her chest.

"Girls, make room for Rosie," I said, wiping away any leftover tears, and Rosie climbed up too. Then Jennica came running over, worried that the chair would collapse, so we piled onto the grass instead. I tickled all three of them and gave them airplane rides, putting my feet on their tummies and lifting them into the air and making airplane noises. Jennica sat close by, and I could tell she didn't one hundred percent trust me, and I guess I couldn't blame her.

As I placed my feet into their chubby little tummies, first Lola, then Lucy, I realized that deep in my heart, I loved my half sisters, I loved them more than I thought I ever could. But I would never love them as much as I loved Rosie.

And maybe it was terrible to think that. But Dr. Belinda Boniface once told me that I had to own my thoughts. So I was owning this one, too.

After Anna Maria went home, Jennica ordered some pizzas for dinner, and we ate outside on a picnic blanket. Then Rosie and I called Mom to let her know we'd arrived safely.

"Is Dudley there?" I couldn't resist asking.

There was a pause before she answered. *"Signs point to yes."*

I rolled my eyes. "Mom, I invented the Magic-8-Ball conversation. Do *not* use it on me."

"Sorry, Violet. Just trying for a bit of levity."

I softened my tone. "Yeah. I know."

"And no, I haven't answered him yet. I've told him I need some time to think."

"You can't marry him, Mom."

"Violet."

I didn't respond.

"Well, I should let you go."

"Mom?"

"Yes?"

"I love you."

"And I love you, my dear silly girl."

—

Dad still wasn't home by the time I went to bed. Rosie was already sound asleep, her little chest rising and falling with each breath, her sheet twisted around her feet.

I read my book for a long time, but it was still hard to concentrate. My thoughts kept drifting to Dudley's proposal, to Jean-Paul, and to Ashley's nose.

And to Phoebe. Especially Phoebe. What a mess I'd made. She was my best friend, and I missed her like crazy.

I heard Dad's car pull up around midnight. I thought about climbing out of bed and meeting him at the door to say hello, but I didn't really feel like it and so I didn't. I knew I would see him in the morning, over breakfast.

I could put my plan into motion then.

— 22 —

Thanks to one tiny beam of sunlight that shone through a crack in our bedroom curtains like a laser beam, directly into my left eye, I woke up early the next morning. Rosie was still sound asleep, so I slipped out of bed and closed the door quietly behind me.

As I approached the kitchen, I could hear voices. Raised voices, arguing. I slowed my pace and strained to hear.

"That's the third new dress in the last month." Dad's voice.

"You know I have to look good when I go to an audition." Jennica's voice.

"Of course. But you have a closetful of outfits to choose from."

"I hate wearing the same thing twice to these things; I feel like I'm jinxing it."

"That . . . is ridiculous."

"And you're one to talk, Mr. I-Just-Bought-a-Brand-New-Mercedes-Benz-Convertible."

"I needed a new car. Besides, this pilot pays well."

"Oh, so just because you're working and I'm not, you're allowed to spend and I need to pinch pennies?"

"That's not what I meant."

"When we first met, *I* was outearning *you*, and did I ever make you feel bad about what you spent?"

"Jennica, be reasonable. We're mortgaged up the wazoo here. This pilot may never go to series. You haven't worked in six months."

"Thanks a lot, Ian. Thanks for the reminder."

I chose that moment to walk into the room. "Good morning," I announced in my best I-have-overheard-nothing voice.

Dad's face lit up. "Violet!" He looked genuinely happy to see me, which surprised me. He wrapped his arms around me and squeezed me tight. I breathed in the scent of him and suddenly felt tears prick my eyes, even though I didn't feel particularly sad.

But all I said was "Hello, Father."

"Look at you. You're hardly a kid anymore. You're turning into a beautiful young woman."

I rolled my eyes. "Please."

"I see more of your mother in you every day."

I wasn't sure how to take that, so I wriggled free and grabbed a bowl from a nearby cupboard. "You have any cereal?"

Jennica got down a bunch of boxes, and, for the first time, I noticed her new outfit. It was a white baby-doll sundress that showed off her assets, if you know what I mean. She wore a lot of makeup that somehow managed to look mostly natural. Mostly.

"You look nice," I told her as I checked out the cereal labels. They were all what my mother would call junk: Cap'n Crunch, Count Chocula, Lucky Charms. I grabbed the box of Lucky Charms.

"Thanks," she said, shooting my dad a look. "I have an audition later this morning."

Dad poured himself a cup of coffee. "I'm sorry I have to work so much while you're here, sweetheart."

I shrugged. "No big deal." Then I said, as casually as possible, "I hear George Clooney's shooting a movie at the same studio."

"That's right. They're on Lot 9. We're on Lot 18."

"Have you met him?"

Dad smiled. "Never even seen him. Tantamount Studios is huge."

My heart sank, but only a little. I poured myself a huge bowl of Lucky Charms. "Can I come to the set with you today?"

Dad's brow furrowed. "Gosh, Violet. I couldn't possibly swing it for today. We're shooting this big action sequence – it's going to be chaos. And not nearly as interesting as you might think."

"Tomorrow, then."

"Tomorrow's not good, either."

"Ian," Jennica said, and her voice had a slight edge to it. "Your daughter would like to see what you do."

It was kind of fun, watching my dad get backed into a corner. "Please, Dad," I said, laying it on a bit thick. "I want to spend more time with you."

"But that's the problem. I won't be able to spend time with *you*. It's go, go, go, from the moment I get there till the moment I leave."

I opened my eyes just a little bit wider and blinked a few times, like I might cry at any moment. "*Please*, Daddy," I said.

He sighed. "Let me check the schedule when I get into work, okay? If there's a day that's not completely insane while you're here, I'll arrange for you to visit. But I'm not making any promises, understood?"

I nodded. It was the most I was going to get out of him for now.

After breakfast, I asked Jennica if I could borrow her computer.

"Sure thing," she said. She brought her MacBook Pro into the living room. I logged on to Facebook. First, I checked Karen's home page. The photos of my mom had been removed. Next, I went under my FRIENDS list to delete Ashley Anderson, but she was already gone. She'd beat me to it.

Just as I was about to shut down, I noticed, under CHAT at the bottom of the page, that one of my friends was online, too. Since I had so few Facebook friends, this hardly ever happened. I clicked on the icon to see who it was.

Phoebe Stegel, it said.

Without taking time to think about it, I typed her a message, hit RETURN, and held my breath.

Violet Gustafson = Butthead. Can you ever forgive me?

I waited. Just when I was convinced she was going to ignore me, a response popped up on the screen.

Violet Gustafson = Phoebe's best friend. One fight isn't going to change that.

Ever since our fight, it felt like a boa constrictor had wrapped itself around my heart. Now, the pressure lifted, and it felt like I could breathe again.

I love you.

Please. Don't go all mooshy on me. I can't believe I missed you hitting Ashley. I was home with a cold. It's all anyone's talking about.

I am not proud.

Nor should you be. So I take it you apologized to your dad?

Yes. But I had a motive.

What?

Dudley asked my mom to marry him.

NO WAY!!! What did she say?

She hasn't answered him yet.

Wow. But – this doesn't explain why you apologized to your dad.

I found out George Clooney is shooting a movie at Tantamount Studios.

The same place your dad is shooting his pilot?

Exactly.

You're going to try to meet George!!

Smart girl. But Dad hasn't agreed to let me visit the set yet. I'm trying to come up with a backup plan.

There was a long pause again. I knew Phoebe was thinking. After a minute, her response popped up.

Star maps.

Star maps?

Those maps they sell of stars' homes. Maybe G.C.'s house is on one.

You're brilliant.

As always. Keep me posted, okay?

But, of course.

Hey. Don't you want to hear about the dance?

I don't know. Do I?

Yes. You do. Ashley and Jean-Paul didn't show.

Really?

Really.

Maybe she didn't want to go with a broken nose.

Maybe. Gotta run, Violet. Cathy's taking me to her chanting class. Bye!! xo

My heart felt so much lighter as I shut down Jennica's computer. Phoebe and I were okay. And buying a star map was a great idea. *But how could I get my hands on one, and, more important, if George Clooney's house was listed, how would I get there?*

Jennica appeared in the doorway. "Violet, Anna Maria just arrived. I should be back by lunch."

A lightbulb went on in my head. "Could I come with you?"

Jennica looked at me like she didn't understand the question.

"To your audition. I mean, not *into* your audition, but . . . I could come, and then afterward we could spend some time together. You know. A girls' afternoon."

As I spoke, Jennica's expression moved from shock to suspicion to what I could only describe as . . . I don't know . . . *joy*. "You want to spend the day . . . with me?" Honestly, she looked like she was about to cry.

"Sure."

"I'd love that. We'll have so much fun. We could go for sushi. And I could book us mani-pedis."

"Whats?"

"A manicure and a pedicure."

"Actually," I said, "I have something else in mind."

"What's that?"

"A driving tour of the stars' homes."

Jennica didn't look thrilled, but all she said was "Sure. We'll do whatever you want. I'll go let Anna Maria know I won't be home till later."

She practically skipped out of the room. I smiled just a little bit. Honestly, it was almost too easy.

Jennica's audition was in Burbank. The traffic was terrible, and it took us over an hour to get there, but we'd left in plenty of time so she wouldn't be late.

I won't lie, it was kind of cool driving down the traffic-congested highways of L.A. in Jennica's VW Golf Convertible. She'd loaned me her sunglasses again, the ones that said LOUIS VUITTON in small letters on their black frames. And while we drove, I pretended I was a movie star being chauffeured to work.

Halfway through the drive, Jennica fumbled around

in her purse and handed me some sheets of paper. "Do you mind running my lines with me?" she asked. "You read the lines I haven't highlighted."

It was a couple of pages from a script for a sitcom called *Couch Potatoes*. I'd seen it once or twice in Vancouver. I didn't think it was very funny, but I didn't tell Jennica that.

I read the Joey and Ramone parts while Jennica read Ally, the part she was auditioning for.

AUDITION SCENE: ALLY

INT. GRIND COFFEE SHOP - DAY

JOEY and RAMONE sit at their favorite table. Joey can't stop ogling a HOT FEMALE PATRON (ALLY).

RAMONE

Dude, close your mouth. Your drool's about to hit your coffee.

JOEY

I can't help it. I'm besotted.

RAMONE

Please, she's old. She must be pushing thirty.

JOEY

So? That's twenty-five in Cougar years.

Joey stands up.

JOEY

I'm gonna talk to her.

RAMONE

Just don't use any of your lame pickup lines on her, Dude.

Joey crosses the room, stands in front of Ally's table. She glances up at him.

ALLY

Can I help you?

JOEY

Yes. I think you stole something that belongs to me.

Ally looks confused and a little pissed off.

ALLY

Excuse me? What on earth do you think I stole from you?

JOEY

My heart.

He smiles winningly. To his delight, Ally actually smiles back.

ALLY

Wow, that was lame. But sweet, too.

JOEY

Do you mind if I join you?

ALLY

I guess that would be okay.

JOEY

What are you drinking?

ALLY

A tall nonfat chai soy latte with a dash of cinnamon.

JOEY

(lying)

No way, that's my favorite too.

(shouting)

Waiter! Two more tall nonfat chai soy lattes with cinnamon, please.

Joey glances across the room at Ramone. Ramone can't believe his pickup lines actually worked this time.

END SCENE

"Wow," I said, after we'd read it through. "Your character sure doesn't have a lot of lines."

"It's just the audition scene," she replied. "It's actually not a bad guest-star role. She winds up being a kleptomaniac who steals Joey's wallet and his computer."

"Still," I said. "It's kind of a step down, isn't it? I mean, you were the star of *Paranormal Pam*."

"For a nanosecond. They pulled it after three episodes, remember?"

"It *was* pretty bad," I said.

She looked startled for a moment, then she burst out laughing. "You're right. I wish my agent had been that honest. Anyway, Violet, this is how the business works. Hot one day, not the next. But I'm an optimist. I know the tides will turn back in my favor at some point."

Jennica found street parking. She spent a few minutes touching up her makeup and combing her hair, then we walked into the building.

The lobby was cool and spacious and full of potted palms and black leather couches. Jennica spoke to the receptionist, who told us to continue on to a room at the far end of the hall.

I admired Jennica's walk as she headed down the hall in her strappy high-heeled sandals. She had such a confident stride. It was like Ashley's walk, except all grown-up. And she had the expression to match. It said *look out world, here I come.*

But when she entered the room, her expression changed. Crammed into the tiny space, on plastic folding chairs, were about fifteen Jennica look-alikes. They all had blonde hair. They all had fake boobs. They all had perfectly straight, blindingly white teeth. And they were all auditioning for the part of Ally.

"I'll wait in the lobby," I said.

"Okay, Violet. This shouldn't take too long."

I was about to pass out from boredom when Jennica finally emerged two hours later.

"Violet, I am *so* sorry. They took forever with some of the girls."

"I'm so hungry, I'm about to gnaw off my own arm."

"C'mon then, screw sushi. I know a great burger joint close to here."

Being L.A., we got in the car to drive a few blocks. A parking ticket fluttered under Jennica's windshield wiper. She cursed under her breath and shoved it into her purse. "Don't tell your dad, okay?"

I nodded. "How'd your audition go?"

"Not great. I was in and out in no time. I think by the time I got in there, they'd already decided on someone else. One of the producers was actually talking on her cell phone during my audition."

"What a jerk."

She smiled at me. "Yes. She was. But you know what? It's nothing some retail therapy won't cure. Let's go shopping after lunch."

"What about our tour of the stars' homes?" I asked, a bubble of panic rising up in my stomach.

"We'll have time for both. Promise. C'mon, let me buy you some new clothes. Starting with a better-fitting swimsuit."

I thought about the fight she'd had with my dad that morning about money. Then I thought about the piles of stuff Lola and Lucy had – the clothes, the toys, the princess room, the pool.

And I said, "Sure!"

I cannot tell a lie. Retail therapy was fun. After we'd wolfed down bacon cheeseburgers and fries, Jennica drove us to one of L.A.'s coolest clothing stores in West Hollywood, Fred Segal. I couldn't believe the prices in there, but Jennica didn't bat an eye, so I let her buy me some new tops and a great pair of jeans. Then she took me to her favorite swimsuit store, and we actually found a one-piece that didn't look half-bad on me.

"It's all about the cut," she said. "It accentuates your gorgeous legs."

"Please. I have man-knees. My legs are hideous."

"Are you kidding me? Women would kill for your legs, Violet. They go on forever."

I had never thought of my legs that way before.

After we left the swimsuit store, Jennica drove us to Hollywood Boulevard, where we bought a map of the stars' homes in a souvenir shop. "Is George Clooney's house on here?" I asked the guy at the counter.

"Yup," he said in a bored voice.

"You like George Clooney?" Jennica asked as we headed back to her car.

"He's alright," I lied. "My mom's a huge fan. I promised her I'd take a photo of his house."

I didn't want her to get suspicious, so I asked her to drive us past other celebrity homes, too. We drove through some incredible neighborhoods, with names I'd heard in songs and on TV: Beverly Hills, Bel Air, Laurel Canyon, Mulholland Drive, Sunset Boulevard. You could barely see a lot of the houses from the road because they had either tall shrubs or security fences to protect them from prying eyes.

After half an hour of this, I asked if we could drive to George Clooney's place. "I don't want to disappoint my mom."

Jennica studied the map for a moment, then she put the car into gear and pulled away from the curb. "I wanted to say thank you, Violet," she said.

"For what?"

"For suggesting we spend the day together. For making an effort. I know how you must feel about me."

I didn't answer.

"And I think that's why you did what you did to Lola and Lucy, right? Because I don't believe for a moment that you'd really want to hurt them." I could hear the doubt in her voice.

I couldn't look at her. I just shook my head as we turned onto George's street.

"I never thought I'd be 'the other woman,' you know. That wasn't part of my life plan, let me tell you." Jennica was saying this as much to herself as she was to me. "I guess I'm hoping that we can turn over a new leaf here, you and me –"

"This is it," I said, cutting her off. "Stop the car."

Jennica pulled over. I opened the door and hopped out. "Back in a flash."

I ran across the street to George's house. Like a lot of the others, it had high shrubs surrounding it. I slipped around the side of the house and tried to squeeze through one of the shrubs, just to see what things looked like on the other side. But beyond the shrubs was a high fence.

I made my way back to the front of the house. A wrought-iron gate blocked the driveway. I needed to get to George's front door, so I tried to push it open. It was locked.

Suddenly someone spoke to me. "Can I help you?" It was a male voice.

I glanced around, startled, but no one was there.

"I said, can I help you?"

That's when I saw the intercom on the fence.

"*Um,* hi," I said, speaking into the intercom. "Is this George?"

"George who?"

"George Clooney."

"Kid, if I was George Clooney, do you think I'd be answering my own intercom?"

"Why not? And how do you know I'm a kid?"

"Look up. Look way, way up."

I did. A camera was perched on top of the wrought-iron fence. I smiled sheepishly and waved.

"Oh. Hi."

"Hi."

"So, is George home?"

"I hate to break it to you, kid. Not only is George Clooney not home, George Clooney does not even live at this address."

"Yes, he does."

The guy laughed. "I can assure you, he doesn't."

"But my star map says –"

"Kid, those star maps are a waste of money. Most of that information is years out of date."

My heart sank. "Really?"

"Really."

From across the street, Jennica started to beep her horn.

"That stinks," I said.

"For you, maybe. For the stars, not so much. Imagine having people drive by your house all day and night, trying to catch a glimpse of you."

"I guess. But I'm not trying to catch a glimpse. I have something important to ask him."

"That's what they all say." He sounded tired. "Now scram, okay? You seem like an okay kid, so don't make me have to call the police."

I nodded. Then I waved at the video camera and walked across the road, sliding back into the passenger seat of Jennica's car.

"What were you doing over there? You could have had us arrested!"

"I told you. I was taking a picture for my mom."

Jennica picked up my camera from the backseat. "Some picture," she said.

"Can we go home?" I asked. "I'm really tired all of a sudden."

Jennica looked at me. I leaned my head against the window, completely discouraged.

"Sure thing," she said eventually. "Let's go home."

When we got back, Rosie and the twins were in the family room, engaged in an elaborate game of "school." Rosie was the teacher and therefore the boss, and she was having a great time telling Lola and Lucy what to do.

After we'd eaten dinner (prepared by Anna Maria before she left for home), Jennica put the twins to bed, and

I put Rosie to bed. Rosie insisted she didn't need a pull-up. "I haven't peed my pants for a week!"

When I was done reading to her, I went to the family room and turned on their enormous flat-screen TV. I couldn't help it – I felt depressed.

Jennica came in a few minutes later. "Violet, your dad just called. He says you and I can visit him on set tomorrow. We'll drive over there in the morning."

My mood lifted. This was it. My best and final chance to meet George Clooney.

I couldn't mess up.

— 23 —

"Jennica Valentine and Violet Popischil. We're visiting Ian Popischil on Lot 18," Jennica said the next morning. We were sitting in her car outside the guard booth at Tantamount Studios.

Pulling into the studio had been pretty cool. First we'd driven under a beautiful art deco archway, with the words *Tantamount Studios* engraved right into the stone. A big fountain, carved out of the same stone, shot up plumes of water just beyond the archway. The surrounding grounds were planted with an incredible array of multicolored tropical plants and flowers. About fifty meters past the fountain, the road was blocked by a guardrail, like the kind they have in parking lots. A security booth sat next to it, and a guard had stepped out to ask who we were visiting.

He stepped back into the booth with Jennica's identification and checked a list. Then he came out a minute later and handed her a security pass.

"And here's a map to guide you," he said, but Jennica waved the map away.

"It's okay. I know my way around."

"I'll take the map," I said quickly. "For a souvenir."

We drove through the studio grounds for what felt like an eternity. The place was huge. We passed low-rise building after low-rise building, and I realized, with a bit of awe, that there was probably a TV show or a movie shooting in every single one of them. We passed an outdoor set that looked exactly like the main street of a small U.S. town and another outdoor set that looked a lot like the Wild West.

And then I saw it: Lot 9. The studio where George Clooney was shooting his movie. I tried to memorize the drive from his lot to ours, but my sense of direction wasn't the greatest. Still, I had the map in my pocket, which would help me find my way back.

A few minutes later, Jennica pulled into a parking spot outside Lot 18. We both got out of the car. "Here we are," she said.

A guy in his twenties was waiting for us at the studio door. He was cute in a scruffy kind of way. "I'm Ben, Ian's assistant. Come on through. We're between setups right now."

He took us down a long corridor. We passed offices and dressing rooms and the hair-and-makeup room, then we stopped at a door that had a large red light over it. I knew from the few times I'd visited Mom and Dad on set when I was younger that when the light is on, it means they're shooting and you aren't supposed to enter. But now the light was off, and we stepped inside.

The set was incredible. It was supposed to be the inside of a high-tech spaceship, and if I didn't look up to see all the lights hanging from the ceiling, and if I ignored the crew members who were setting up for the next scene, I could almost believe that I'd been abducted by aliens.

Then I saw my dad, standing by the snack table. He was talking to a pretty redheaded woman. Judging by her outfit, a *Star Trek*-style clingy one-piece space suit, I guessed she was one of his actresses. His hand rested casually on her arm.

I looked at Jennica. She, too, had spotted my dad.

"If I were you?" I told her. "I'd visit Dad again sometime. But next time, I'd show up unannounced."

Jennica looked at me sharply and opened her mouth to say something. But she must have realized I'd only said it to be helpful because she didn't say whatever she was going to say. Instead, she brushed her hand gently against my cheek. "Eyelash," she said.

And suddenly I felt a great wave of sympathy for her because, let's face it, if Dad could cheat on his first wife, he could cheat on his second wife, too.

"And . . . cut!" Dad shouted from his director's chair behind the monitor. It was a fancy black canvas chair, with his name stitched on the back and a drink holder and everything. I sat behind him, also in a black canvas chair, but without the name or the cup holder. I wore a headset so I could hear the dialogue clearly. Jennica had disappeared to have a chat with the wardrobe lady, who'd worked on another show with her.

It had been a mildly interesting couple of hours, even though it was very repetitive, watching the same scene over and over again as it got shot from different angles. Still, it was a good scene – "The one just before the spaceship crash-lands on a strange, hostile planet," Ben told me – and I had to admit, I felt pretty proud of my dad. From what I could tell, he was good at what he did, and the cast and crew obviously liked him.

At one point, though, a guy in a suit showed up and talked to Dad between setups, and that seemed to stress him out.

"One of the producers," Ben explained to me. "We're shooting a lot of overtime, and that costs money, which means we've gone over budget, and your dad's taking the heat for it."

Now, as I sat behind him, Dad consulted with his director of photography and the script supervisor. Then he told his first assistant director, "We're moving on."

The first A.D. shouted out to everyone, "Moving on, folks! We're blocking scene fifteen!"

Dad stood up and turned to me. "I need to rehearse this scene with the actors before we break for lunch, honey. I thought Ben could show you around our outdoor sets in the meantime."

"Sure."

Ben took me outside and ushered me toward a golf cart that was parked nearby. "Hop in."

"Can't we just walk?"

"We could, but we'd never make it back in time for lunch."

Ben drove me past their outdoor sets, which were unbelievable. A huge spaceship wreck had been constructed near the studio. Beyond that were the remains of a destroyed, intergalactic city.

But while it was all very impressive, I had other things on my mind. "Where's Lot 9 from here?" I asked as casually as I could.

"About five minutes thataway," he said, pointing down the road.

"How long would it take to get there on foot?"

"Fifteen minutes, probably. How come?"

"Just curious."

Ben brought me back just as the cast and crew broke for lunch. I wasn't very hungry since I'd pigged out on the craft service snacks all morning. Dad and Jennica were sitting at a table, already eating.

"Grab some food and join us, Violet," Dad said. "The chicken's fantastic."

"We'll head home after lunch," added Jennica.

My heart skipped a beat. "Why? I want to stay longer."

"We can't. Anna Maria has to leave by four today."

"So I'll stay with Dad."

"No can do, hon," he said. "I'm going to be here till at least midnight."

"So? I'm not a baby, I can stay up till then –"

"Violet, the answer is no," Dad said, suddenly sounding stressed. I saw why: The guy in the suit was in the doorway, motioning to my dad to join him.

"Sorry, girls, I'll be right back." He got up and joined the guy in the suit, who waved his hands around a lot as he talked.

I had to think fast. Dad would probably never let me visit him on set again while I was here. If I was going to try to meet George, it was now or never.

I turned to Jennica. "Back in a moment. I need to pee."

I walked down the long corridor, passed the washrooms, and stepped outside. I pulled out the map to get my bearings. If Ben was right, it would take me fifteen minutes on foot to get to Lot 9 and fifteen minutes to get back. Plus I needed time to track down George and talk to him. I'd never get back before Dad's hour-long lunch ended.

Then my gaze landed on Ben's golf cart.

The keys were in the ignition.

— 24 —

It's surprisingly easy to drive a golf cart, I thought, as I cruised down the Tantamount Studios roads. Thankfully there was hardly any traffic, so it didn't matter if I veered around a little when I looked down to double-check the map. I was pretty sure I was going the right way until I saw Lot 1 and realized I'd somehow wound up on the other side of the studio property.

I hadn't figured out how to back up the golf cart, so I did a U-turn instead and headed back the way I'd come. I looked at my watch: I'd already wasted fifteen minutes. According to Ben, I could have walked to Lot 9 in that time. I gunned the engine, making it go at top speed, which, for the golf cart, was about twenty kilometers an hour.

And then, like a beacon in the distance, I saw it.

Lot 9! I sped down the road toward it, when suddenly, from out of nowhere, two live camels walked onto the road, right into my path.

Live camels! I thought I was hallucinating. I swerved as hard as I could to the left – and almost careened into ten belly dancers, walking behind the camels. It was like being in a movie, but it wasn't a movie, it was just stuff *for* a movie. I swerved as hard as I could to the right –

And smashed into a very expensive-looking sports car parked near the entrance to Lot 9.

The last thing I remembered was the golf cart tipping . . .

Me, tumbling out of the golf cart . . .

The sharp, searing sensation of my flesh, skidding across the asphalt . . .

And the golf cart, landing on top of me.

— 25 —

I guess I must have passed out because the next thing I remembered, I was lying on a cot in a sterile white room. I could hear voices nearby.

"*This* is the person who hit my car?" It was a deep, masculine voice.

"Uh-huh." A female voice. I opened my eyes. The female voice belonged to a woman in a white lab coat. I couldn't see the owner of the male voice.

"With a golf cart?"

"Yup. A couple of extras in belly-dancing costumes saw it happen."

"Is she going to be okay?"

"She's got a twisted ankle and some nasty road burn, and we'll have to watch for concussion, but other than that, she should be fine."

"Who is she? Where did she come from?"

"That's what we're trying to find out."

I turned my head left and right, trying to find the owner of the male voice, but he wasn't in my immediate line of vision. I tried lifting myself up, but my head felt like a bowling ball.

"Her eyes are open, Doctor. Could I speak to her for a moment?"

"Be my guest."

Suddenly a male face loomed over me. It was a very handsome face, even if it was a face that belonged to a man who was old enough to be my father. Correction: It was a *very, very, very* handsome face, with warm mischievous eyes and a killer smile.

It was George Clooney.

"Hi, there."

"Hi."

"How are you feeling?"

"Sore."

"The doctor says you'll be fine."

I nodded.

"You hit my car."

I winced. "That was your car?"

He nodded.

"I'm really sorry. I was trying to avoid the camels. And the belly dancers."

"Well, better my car than the camels or the belly

dancers. But if you don't mind my saying so, you look a little young to be driving."

"I'll be old enough soon."

"How soon?"

I hesitated. "Three and a quarter years?"

"*Hmm*. So, let me ask you this: What on earth were you doing, driving one of the studio golf carts?"

"I was coming to visit you."

"You were, were you."

"I wrote you a letter. Two, in fact. You haven't responded yet. I sent them to your manager's address."

"And what did these letters say?"

"I asked if you'd like to meet my mom."

"Your mom?"

"You met her once before, years ago. Ingrid Gustafson?"

He looked at me blankly.

"You wrote on the picture you gave her that you hoped your paths would cross again. I was trying to make that happen."

"Can I ask why?"

"I thought she'd be the type of woman who might change your mind about marriage."

George thought about this for a moment. "I take it your dad isn't in the picture."

"Oh, he's in the picture. Just not with my mom. He's directing a pilot on Lot 18. He's remarried."

"Did your mom put you up to this?"

"No, no. She doesn't know I wrote the letters. She thinks she's perfectly happy dating this man named Dudley Wiener."

"Wiener. Unfortunate name."

"Yes."

"But maybe she is. Happy, I mean."

"No. She's delusional."

"Really."

"Really. He's not good enough for her."

"Why not?"

"Because. He's bland. And balding. And he's a punster. And he's got man-boobs."

"Man-boobs, huh? Well, if you don't mind my saying so, those don't sound like very good reasons. Those sound like, *um*, superficial reasons."

"It's more than that. He's not . . ." I struggled to put it into words. "He's not . . ."

"He's not your dad?"

I nodded, and suddenly my eyes welled up with tears. I was crying, right there in front of George Clooney, big fat tears rolling down my face. "I mean, I know my dad was a jerk in the end, leaving my mom for Wife Number Two and all . . . but when he was really our dad, he was great, you know? Dudley is so . . ."

"Not your dad."

"Not even close." I sniffed back a large snot-ball that had formed in my left nostril.

George handed me a Kleenex and patted my hand.

"See? You're handsome *and* smart *and* kind. You'd be perfect for her."

He shook his head. "I wouldn't."

"Why not?"

"It sounds to me like your mom deserves someone who'd be there for her, always. I'm not that guy."

"Maybe you are that guy, and you just haven't met the right woman."

"It's possible. But I doubt it. A man tends to know himself pretty well when he reaches almost half a century."

"Wow. You're old."

He smiled. "Ancient." He picked up my hand and gave it a gentle squeeze. "Can I tell you something? No one is ever going to be able to replace your dad. Not even me."

I nodded, and my head felt like it might explode.

"But let me ask you this. Does this Wiener guy make your mom happy?"

"It would seem so, yes."

"So maybe you need to give him a chance."

A wave of exhaustion washed over me. I suddenly felt like I could sleep forever.

"What's your name?" asked George.

"Violet. Violet Gustafson." And then, just like that, with the biggest movie star of all time standing over my bed, I fell back into a deep sleep.

— 26 —

When I woke up again, it was pitch-dark, and Jennica was shaking me awake. It took me a full minute to realize I was in my bed at Dad and Jennica's and that Rosie was sound asleep in the bed beside me.

"What are you doing?" I mumbled to Jennica, my voice thick with sleep. I could feel pain pulsing down the right side of my body.

"I have to wake you up once an hour and check your pupils to make sure you don't have a concussion. Doctor's orders."

"Where's Dad?"

"Still at work." I glanced at the clock. It was almost 2:00 a.m. "They shut down production for a couple of hours when he found out you were in the Tantamount infirmary. . . . Once we all realized you'd be okay, he had to rush back and play catch-up."

I thought about the guy in the suit who was already giving my dad grief and groaned. "Dad's gonna be furious."

Jennica squeezed my hand, but she didn't contradict me. "We'll talk about all of this in the morning. In the meantime, I'm just glad you're okay." She stood up and walked to the door. "See you in an hour."

"Jennica?" I said.

She turned back.

"Thanks."

She gave me a small, tired smile before she walked away.

"George Clooney's car!" Dad was pacing back and forth in the kitchen, clutching a mug of coffee.

Jennica and I were still in our pajamas. She had dark circles under her eyes, thanks to her once-an-hour vigil over yours truly the night before. I had a single crutch to help me move around on my twisted ankle. The right side of my body – leg, hip, and arm – was raw and red and starting to form scabs.

"You hit George Clooney's car! With a studio golf cart! That you *stole!* And you're *twelve!*"

"Almost thirteen. And I didn't steal it, I borrowed it –"

"George Clooney's car!" This particular piece of information was clearly the worst part of it for Dad. "He must be furious."

"Not really," I said.

"What do you mean, 'not really'?"

"I spoke with him. In the infirmary."

My dad rubbed his temples. "Violet, don't be ridiculous. George was shooting all day, he couldn't have visited you in the infirmary."

"But he did. Just ask the doctor. She was there."

Jennica said gently, "The doctor wasn't a *she,* Violet. His name was Bernard."

Now I felt confused. "But I *did* talk to him –"

"You'd hit your head. You were hallucinating," my dad said.

"If I was hallucinating, how come I already knew I'd hit his car?"

"Because the parking spot had RESERVED FOR GEORGE CLOONEY painted on the curbstone in enormous letters. You must have seen it while you were lying there on the pavement. . . ." His voice broke. "Violet, you could have killed yourself. You had us worried half to death."

Then he grabbed me and hugged me tightly for a few seconds before letting me go. "Dammit, why can't we ever have a normal visit with you?" He gave Jennica a quick kiss on the crown of her head. "I'm sorry, I have to go. Call time's not for two hours, but I have to revise my storyboard, try to make up for lost time." He shot me a look as he said this.

As he headed out of the room, he shouted over his shoulder, "And call your mother!"

Jennica and I were left alone in the kitchen. We could hear Rosie and the twins, playing happily in the family room. Jennica handed me a pill, something the doctor had given me for the pain. I drank it down with some apple juice.

"Do you really think you saw George Clooney?" she asked.

"Yes. At least, I thought I did. Now I'm not so sure."

"Is he as good-looking in real life as he is in his movies?"

"Better."

Jennica smiled, and the smile turned into a yawn.

"Why don't you go back to bed?" I said.

"I can't. It's Anna Maria's day off."

"I can watch Rosie and the twins," I told her.

She looked at me, and I knew she was trying to decide whether or not she could trust me.

"Just for an hour. And I won't take them outside. We'll stay in the family room." Then I said what she really wanted to hear. "I won't do anything mean. I promise."

She studied my face for a moment. "Okay. Thanks, Violet, I appreciate it." Then she handed me the portable phone. "But first, call your mother."

"Violet, is everything okay?" my mom asked, when I got through to her on her cell phone. She was at work, and I could hear voices in the background.

"Everything's great, Mom. Me and Rosie are fine." I paused. "But I did have a bit of an accident yesterday."

There was silence for a moment. "An accident?"

"I'm fine. I just have a twisted ankle. And I'm pretty scraped up. And they thought I might have a concussion, but I don't."

"What happened?" There was a hint of hysteria in her voice.

"*Um* . . . I kind of fell out of a golf cart. And it kind of landed on top of me."

"What?"

"But, you know, it's a pretty long story, and you're at work and all, so it can wait till I get home –"

"No. No, it can't wait till you get home. Karen, take over for me, will you?"

A moment later, the background noise died down, and I knew she'd stepped into the hall. "Okay, Violet. Tell me everything."

So I did.

— 27 —

“osie, stop squirming.”

“The tag is itchy!”

“Fine, I’ll find someone with scissors.”

It was June. Rosie and I had been home from Los Angeles for three months. And now, here we were, wearing matching bridesmaids dresses. Only technically we weren’t bridesmaids, we were flower girls.

For someone who doesn’t like to wear dresses, I have to admit that these ones were okay. They were simple, with empire waists. The fabric was a silky pearl gray. They stopped just above the knee. My leg was completely healed, the scabs long gone. I remembered what Jennica had said about my legs, and for once in my life, I thought I didn’t look half-bad.

“Karen, do you have scissors?” I asked. She was

wearing the grown-up version of our dress, in the same fabric, but hers was long, form-fitting, and sleeveless. She'd toned down on the makeup, and she actually looked almost pretty.

"Yes, I think I do," she said, rummaging through her handbag. "Here."

I cut Rosie's tag off, and she breathed a sigh of relief. "Better!"

"Here are your baskets," said Karen, handing us each a straw basket full of rose petals. "Remember, and, Rosie, this goes especially for you, don't throw them all at once. Just toss small handfuls as you walk down the aisle."

I nodded, suddenly nervous. The church was packed, and we would be the first two people down the aisle.

But allow me to backtrack for a moment. A lot has happened in the three months since we've been back from L.A.

A lot. And it all started on the night we got home.

My mom picked us up at the airport, but she and I didn't really have a chance to talk until later that night because Rosie had talked a mile a minute from the moment we'd stepped into Mom's car till the moment she'd gone to bed.

It wasn't until we'd pulled up outside our house that I realized the muffler wasn't making any noise.

And, as we climbed the steps, I noticed that the love seat that had sat rotting on our front porch for a year and a half was gone. And the handrail didn't wobble anymore.

After Rosie was asleep, Mom made us hot chocolate. We sat at either end of the red couch in the living room, facing each other, feet touching.

"So," my mom said. "George Clooney." She started to snort with laughter. I didn't think it was *that* funny, but I wasn't going to argue because I was relieved I wasn't in serious trouble. "I can't believe you tried to set me up with *George Clooney*." She had to wipe tears from her eyes, she was laughing so hard. "I suppose I ought to be flattered. But I'm also furious, of course. You stole a golf cart. You drove under age. We'll have to think of a suitable punishment."

So much for not being in serious trouble.

"Aside from trying to set me up with George Clooney," she continued, "how was the rest of your visit?"

"Not bad," I said, and I meant it. I told Mom that after the golf cart incident, Dad and Jennica had taken me, Rosie, Lola, and Lucy to Disneyland for a day, and even though I'd had to hobble around on my crutch, and we'd had to stick to the kiddy rides, it was still really fun. I told her that later in the week, Jennica took us down to the Santa Monica Pier and to Venice Beach, where I was almost positive I saw one of the Olsen twins, but she was on Rollerblades and mostly a blur so it was hard to know for sure.

I told her that we spent a lot of time by Dad's pool and that I went into the water every day in my new bathing suit.

I even told her about my breakfast with Dad.

What happened was this: The day before we left, I'd walked into the kitchen to grab some cereal. Dad was at the counter drinking coffee. "Violet, why don't you and I go out for breakfast?"

"Aren't you shooting today?"

"Call time isn't till noon."

"What about Rosie?"

"She can stay here with the twins."

So Dad took me to a cool little diner down on Venice Beach, where we ate *huevos rancheros* and drank enormous fruit smoothies. Then we walked along the boardwalk, and he bought me a T-shirt and a ball cap and some flip-flops to bring home to Mom.

We were walking back to the house when he said, "I know I haven't been a great father to you lately, Violet."

I didn't know what to say. I focused on the row of palm trees that lined the sidewalk.

"And I know . . . when I left your mom . . . I left you too, in a way. And your sister. I didn't mean to. But I did."

I kept staring at those palm trees.

"I thought I could still be a good father to you. But I guess I haven't done a very good job, after all."

I couldn't be sure, but I think he was waiting for me to say that wasn't true. I didn't.

"Anyway. I guess I just want you to know . . . I'll try harder from now on."

I nodded. I knew he meant it, but I also knew in my heart that I probably shouldn't expect things to change too much.

He cleared his throat. "And maybe you can try a little harder, too. You know, don't steal any more golf carts. Talk to me without the Magic 8 Ball when I call. Do you think you can do that?"

I was quiet for a moment. Then I said, *"Signs point to yes."*

It took him a moment to get it. Then he laughed.

Mom laughed too, when I was done telling her. "Well. Good. I'm glad you two had a chance to talk. And I'm delighted that you had a good time. You ready for your ointment?"

I nodded. She gently pulled off my sweatpants, which were all I could wear since the accident because I couldn't have any fabric rubbing up against my skin. I suddenly felt overwhelmingly happy to be home.

But, of course, I had one burning question. "Did you give Dudley an answer?"

My mom nodded. I held my breath.

"I told him no."

I exhaled, relieved.

"I don't feel ready to go down that path again, at least, not anytime soon."

"Thank you, thank you, thank you!"

"But, Violet . . ." She stopped rubbing the ointment into my leg for a moment and took my hand. "I really like him. I know I made some terrible choices early on, but Dudley is different. All I ask is that you give him a chance. Because I think, if you do that, you'll see that he's quite a wonderful human being. He may not be the cutest, or the richest –"

"Or the funniest –"

"But he makes me happy." Then she added, "Happier in some ways than your dad ever did."

Even though I was sorely tempted, I didn't slap my hands over my ears and sing *"La-la-la-la-la-la-la-la-la"* this time.

"I love you and Rosie with all my heart. But I need a different kind of love, too. Just like you'll need a different kind of love when you get older, something Rosie and I won't be able to provide."

"I'm never falling in love," I said, thinking of Jean-Paul. "It's too much trouble."

Mom smiled. "Well, I hope you change your mind someday. A certain amount of pain is part of life. You can't stop opening yourself up to people and taking chances just because you're scared of getting hurt."

When she'd finished rubbing the ointment into my leg, she said, "Oh, I almost forgot. A boy called here for you, the day after you left."

My heart did a flip. "Who was it?"

"I don't know," she said. "He wouldn't leave a message."

On Sunday – our last day of freedom before school started again after March Break – Phoebe and I spent the whole day together. I filled her in on all that had happened, and when I was done, she shared her theory with me, which went like this: I'd chosen George Clooney as the perfect guy for my mom because I knew, deep in my heart, that I was pursuing an impossible goal. "And that was the point," she said matter-of-factly. "Because you didn't want *anyone*, not even George Clooney, to replace your dad." I had to take her word for it because Phoebe is very smart about these things.

On Monday morning, as we walked (and I hobbled) to school with Rosie, Phoebe still couldn't stop talking about my so-called encounter with George. I was wearing one of my new L.A. shirts, but my pants were the same old sweats I'd been wearing since I got home, thanks to my scabs.

"I think you really saw him," Phoebe said firmly.

"I do, too," I replied.

"Then again," she continued, "your dad could be right. You could have been hallucinating."

"Yeah, it's possible," I said.

"Tell me again what he said. Don't leave anything out."

So I told her everything George Clooney had said, or hadn't said, for the hundredth time.

We dropped Rosie off at kindergarten, then Phoebe and I climbed the stairs to the second floor. I won't lie; I felt like barfing. There were a lot of people I wasn't looking forward to facing on my first day back at school.

First up: Thing One. She was at her locker, between us and the classroom, and there was no avoiding her. She had tape across her nose.

Phoebe squeezed my shoulder. "Good luck," she said. I took a deep breath and approached her.

"Ashley –" I started.

"Keep away from me," she snapped.

"I just wanted to say I'm really sorry. What you did was really horrible. But I never should have hit you."

She just slammed her locker shut. "Don't come near me ever again, Pancake."

Lauren marched up beside her, arms crossed over her chest. "You heard her, Psycho."

I thought about pleading my case, but I knew there was no point. So I walked away. I could feel a lot of eyes on me in the hall. Phoebe joined me. "You did what you could," she said.

I nodded, but the truth was, I felt pretty shaken. "I'll see you in class," I told her. "I have to drop off some overdue books."

As I entered the library, I almost walked right into Jean-Paul.

"Hey, *Pamplemousse*."

"Hi, Jean-Paul." I looked at my feet, feeling generally, all-around mortified.

"What happened to you?" he asked, indicating the scabs on my arm.

"It's a long story."

"I'd like to hear it sometime. Did you have a good March Break?"

"Yeah, I did. How about you?"

"It was good. I spent it in Winnipeg with my dad."

I kept looking at my feet. It was all very awkward.

"I didn't go to the dance," he said. "I told Ashley to forget it. I didn't want to go with her after what she did to you. I tried to call you, but you'd already left."

I just could not make myself look up from my shoes.

"I was wondering," he continued, "if maybe this weekend we could do something, like see a movie, or . . . something. We could ask Phoebe and Andrew to come, too."

I finally tore my gaze away from my feet, even though I knew he'd see my full-on blush. "I'd like that," I replied.

We went to a movie that weekend, the four of us. And the next weekend, Jean-Paul and I went to the aquarium, just the two of us. We've been sort-of, kind-of dating ever since. Last weekend he came over to our house for the official Gustafson Girls' Night, which I think we're going to have to rename because it's never just girls anymore, and we all watched *Ocean's 13*, starring you-know-who. Dudley was there too, and he and my mom kept giggling whenever George was on-screen.

"If George ever did come calling," Dudley asked my mom, "what would you do?"

"What do you think?" my mom replied. "I'd let him in!"

Jean-Paul held my hand during the whole movie, right in front of everyone. Rosie took turns leaning against him and leaning against Dudley. She didn't put her thumb in her mouth once.

Jean-Paul is spending the summer in Winnipeg. We've promised we'll e-mail each other every day. *Do I worry that he'll meet someone else?* Yes. *Do I worry that my heart will wind up getting crushed?* Totally.

But I'm also starting to come around to what Mom said. You have to be open to new experiences. You have to take the bad with the good.

That's life, after all.

The music started. Cosmo stood at the front, looking drop-dead gorgeous in a tuxedo. His best man, if you could call him a man, stood beside him. I'd met him at the rehearsal dinner the night before. His name was Ambrose, and he couldn't have been much older than me.

"Violet," he'd said when we were introduced. "*Olive, evil, live, volt, veil, veto, vole, love.*" Seriously, he said that. "They're anagrams," he explained. "Using some of the letters from your name."

What can I say? Weird with a capital *W*.

The crowd rose to their feet. Rosie and I started down the aisle, tossing petals as we went. Phoebe caught my eye and winked at me. And Dudley – who, I must admit, looked almost handsome in his suit – gave us both two thumbs-up.

We stood at the front and watched as my mom came down the aisle, followed by Karen and another friend of Amanda's. Mom wore the same dress as Karen, and she looked fantastic. I swear I saw Dudley's chest puff out with pride as she passed him. I won't lie, I still thought he was a dork. But as Phoebe likes to point out, there are worse qualities than dorkiness.

And, thanks to him, I'd managed to get a *B* on my last math test. I'd finally relented and let him help me study one night. If I'm honest, he was a pretty good teacher, way better than Mr. Patil. It was like I'd been struggling to learn a new language, and somehow Dudley helped me crack the code, and the math started to make sense. He'd been in the middle of explaining something to me when I'd interrupted him. "If you hurt my mom, I'll have to kill you," I said, not glancing up from my math book.

"Coming from any other kid, I would take this as an idle threat. But from you . . . ," he said. "Seriously, Violet. I'm not going to hurt your mom."

"But how do I know?"

He shrugged. "You don't, I guess. You just have to trust me."

Trust. That's something I've been trying to work on. And looking at Cosmo as he waited anxiously to see his bride, I had to trust that he and Amanda would do just fine. Maybe with some bumps along the way, but still.

The music swelled, and Amanda appeared on her dad's arm. Her dress was long, off-white, simple but elegant. Her hair was swept up into a bun on top of her head. She looked gorgeous.

When the bride and groom said "I do," the entire church erupted into cheers. And I cheered, too.

Oh, I almost forgot.

Something else happened, about two weeks after I got home. A brown envelope arrived in the mail, addressed to me, from the office of George Clooney. This is what it said.

> Dear **Violet**,
>
> Thank you for your fan letter to George Clooney. Unfortunately, due to the volume of fan mail he receives, we must respond with a form letter.
>
> However, please be assured that George appreciates the time you took to write to him, and as an expression of his gratitude, we have enclosed a signed eight-by-ten glossy of him for your collection.
>
> Sincerely,
>
> The Office of George Clooney

After I'd read the form letter, I slid the photograph out of the envelope. It was the same one his office had sent the first time, a head shot of George, looking right at me, smiling that amazing smile.

Only this time, something was written in the bottom right-hand corner.

To Violet –
A better daughter than she is a driver.
Best wishes,
George Clooney